"You want to offer me a job?"
Kate asked, staring at Marsh in disbelief at his words.

"It's only for a day or two at the most. I'd very much appreciate it if you could see your way to helping me out." Marsh's tone was warm and persuasive. "I'm not asking for myself. I'm asking for my daughter."

Kate heard his underlying cry for help, and she could see his anxiety. She knew she should tell Marsh she couldn't work for him for any price, but the words stuck in her throat. She didn't belong in his world—never had and never would. Still, his home had always touched a chord somewhere deep inside her. It was the only place that had ever made Kate feel like she was coming home.

"So will you be coming home with us, Kate?"

"Yes, I'm coming," Kate said, unable to find it in her heart to say no.

Dear Reader,

The end of the century is near, and we're all eagerly anticipating the wonders to come. But no matter what happens, I believe that everyone will continue to need and to seek the unquenchable spirit of love…of *romance*. And here at Silhouette Romance, we're delighted to present another month's worth of terrific, emotional stories.

This month, RITA Award-winning author Marie Ferrarella offers a tender BUNDLES OF JOY tale, in which *The Baby Beneath the Mistletoe* brings together a man who's lost his faith and a woman who challenges him to take a chance at love…and family. In Charlotte Maclay's charming new novel, a millionaire playboy isn't sure what he was *Expecting at Christmas,* but what he gets is a *very* pregnant butler! Elizabeth Harbison launches her wonderful new theme-based miniseries, CINDERELLA BRIDES, with the fairy-tale romance—complete with mistaken identity!—between *Emma and the Earl*.

In *A Diamond for Kate* by Moyra Tarling, discover whether a doctor makes his devoted nurse his devoted wife *after* learning about her past…. Patricia Thayer's cross-line miniseries WITH THESE RINGS returns to Romance and poses the question: Can *The Man, the Ring, the Wedding* end a fifty-year-old curse? You'll have to read this dramatic story to find out! And though *The Millionaire's Proposition* involves making a baby in Natalie Patrick's upbeat Romance, can a down-on-her-luck waitress also convince him to make beautiful memories…as man and wife?

Enjoy this month's offerings, and look forward to a new century of timeless, traditional tales guaranteed to touch your heart!

Mary-Theresa Hussey

Mary-Theresa Hussey
Senior Editor, Silhouette Romance

Please address questions and book requests to:
Silhouette Reader Service
U.S.: 3010 Walden Ave., P.O. Box 1325, Buffalo, NY 14269
Canadian: P.O. Box 609, Fort Erie, Ont. L2A 5X3

A DIAMOND
FOR KATE

Moyra Tarling

Silhouette
R O M A N C E™
Published by Silhouette Books
America's Publisher of Contemporary Romance

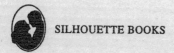

SILHOUETTE BOOKS

ISBN 0-373-19411-0

A DIAMOND FOR KATE

Copyright © 1999 by Moyra Tarling

Visit us at www.romance.net

Printed in U.S.A.

Books by Moyra Tarling

Silhouette Romance

MOYRA TARLING

was born and raised in Aberdeenshire, Scotland. It was there that she was first introduced to and became hooked on romance novels. In 1968, she immigrated to Vancouver, Canada, where she met and married her husband. They have two grown children. Empty-nesters now, they enjoy taking trips in their getaway van and browsing in antique shops for corkscrews and button-hooks. But Moyra's favorite pastime is curling up with a great book—a romance, of course! Moyra loves to hear from readers. You can write to her at P.O. Box 161, Blaine, WA 98231-D161.

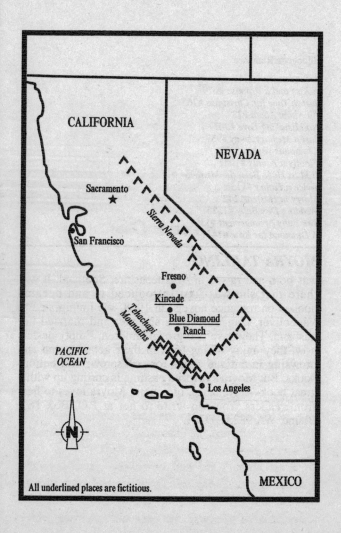

CALIFORNIA

NEVADA

Sacramento ★

San Francisco

Sierra Nevada

Fresno

Kincade

Blue Diamond
Ranch

Tehachapi
Mountains

PACIFIC
OCEAN

Los Angeles

N

MEXICO

All underlined places are fictitious.

Chapter One

"It's Dr. Diamond!" Nurse Kate Turner exclaimed, instantly recognizing the unconscious man the ambulance crew had just wheeled in. Even though she hadn't seen him in ten years, she'd have known Marsh anywhere. His indelibly handsome image was etched in her memory.

"Who?" asked the first attendant, as he maneuvered the stretcher into the first trauma room.

"Dr. Marshall Diamond," Kate repeated. "Mercy Hospital's new chief of staff."

Ever since Kate had heard the news several weeks ago that Marshall Diamond had been hired as the new chief of staff for Mercy Hospital, she'd wondered if she was the only one in town who wasn't cheering his return or rolling out the red carpet.

"What have we here?" Dr. Tom Franklin, head of the Emergency Department, asked as he joined them.

"Car accident victim," the attendant replied. "A teenage driver ran the red light at Cutter's Junction and rammed into the driver's side of this guy's car. He's got a head injury, possible fracture of the left arm and various cuts and bruises. Nurse here says the victim is one of yours, a Dr. Diamond."

"My God! She's right," Dr. Franklin said in a shocked voice. "Okay, team. On the count of three let's move him over."

Kate and the other staff members in the room lifted Marsh from the stretcher to the hospital bed.

An array of emotions swept through Kate as her gaze once more came to rest on Marsh's bloodied face. She focused her scattered thoughts and proceeded to clean the facial injuries, wiping away the blood seeping from a deep cut just below his hairline.

"That looks nasty," Dr. Franklin commented. "And there's a swelling above his right eye. He must have hit the steering wheel," he added as he studied the wound. "That cut will definitely need stitching. Has he regained consciousness at all?"

"Yes, but only for a few seconds," the attendant replied. "He was disoriented and mumbling something about his daughter. She was belted into the passenger seat and appeared to be all right. He took the brunt of the collision."

"Thanks. We'll take it from here," Dr. Franklin said. "Kate, once you're finished cleaning that wound, I'll put in a few sutures to close it. When I'm done, Jackie can take him upstairs to X-ray his left wrist. We're probably looking at a possible concussion. Kate, alert X ray, and tell them to give this top priority. I want to see those films, stat."

"Yes, doctor," Kate replied.

While Dr. Franklin continued his examination, Kate finished up in the room and then went to the phone at the nurses' desk.

"I'm taking Dr. Diamond up now," said Jackie Gibson, another Emergency nurse, as she wheeled the gurney into the hallway. "I'll be right back."

"Fine," Kate replied. "Oh, Jackie, one of the ambulance guys said the doctor's daughter was in the car with him. Has she been brought in yet?"

"I think she just arrived."

Kate spun around to see a policeman, carrying a child of about five years old, wearing red shorts and a yellow T-shirt, and hugging a teddy bear. She had shoulder-length hair the color of corn silk, and it was obvious from her blotchy face and tear-stained cheeks she'd been crying.

"Is this the little girl from the accident?" Kate asked, glimpsing fear in the child's eyes.

"Yes," the policeman confirmed. "How's her father doing?"

"He's on his way up to X ray. Is she hurt?"

"I don't think so. But you'd better check her over just to make sure."

"Here, let me take her." Kate lifted the child into her arms and crossed to one of the curtained beds.

"Lucky for her she was wearing her seat belt," the policeman said, following beside them. "Uh...listen, nurse. While you take care of her, I'll give my sergeant at the station a call."

"Sure, go ahead," Kate said as she gently lowered the girl onto the bed.

"Who have we here?" asked Dr. Davis, one of the E.R. residents.

"Can you tell us your name?" Kate asked.

"Sa...Sabrina Diamond," came the ragged reply.

"Sabrina. That's a lovely name," Kate responded warmly. "I'm Kate.

Dr. Davis approached the bed and flashed the child a kindly smile.

"Sabrina and her father were in a car accident," Kate went on. "She appears to be all right."

"Let's take a quick look shall we?" Dr. Davis said.

Kate stood by while the doctor examined the child.

"You're a very lucky girl, Sabrina," Dr. Davis finally said, but the child made no response, simply hugging her teddy bear tighter. He turned to Kate and lowered his voice. "Find out how her father is doing and then contact any family."

After the doctor departed, Kate studied her patient more closely, noting that her eyes were the same startling blue as her father's. She even had the same serious look about her, but there was also a deep sadness in Sabrina's eyes that tugged at her heart. She knew the child's mother had died in a boating accident several months ago. At the time Kate had felt an affinity with the five-year-old, having lost her own mother when she'd been the same age.

"I know it must have been scary for you being in an accident. But Dr. Davis says you're just fine." Reaching for a box of tissues beside the bed, she wiped a stray tear from the girl's face.

While there was no visible evidence of any physical injury, Kate knew that being in the accident, seeing a loved one bleeding and unconscious beside her had to have been a highly traumatic experience for the child.

"Is my daddy dead?" The question was asked in a voice that quavered with emotion.

"No. But he was hurt in the accident." She kept her tone even, then watched helplessly as Sabrina's eyes filled with fresh tears.

"Can I see him?"

"He's been taken upstairs for X rays."

"What's an X ray?"

"Your daddy might have broken his arm in the accident. An X ray is a machine that can take pictures of his bones to see if any are broken," she explained, fighting the urge to reach out and pull the child into her arms.

"Does it hurt?"

Kate smiled. "No, X rays don't hurt."

"When can I see him?"

"I don't know if..." Kate began, and immediately regretted her words, as the tears hovering on Sabrina's lashes spilled over to cascade down her pale cheeks.

"Aw...sweetheart, don't cry." Kate grabbed more tissues from the box and wiped away the tears. "Your father's being well looked after, I promise you."

The child's lower lip continued to tremble. "I

want to see my daddy,'' she stated emphatically before burying her face against her teddy bear.

Kate put her arm around Sabrina's shoulder, easily understanding the child's need to see her father. No doubt, with the loss of her mother still fresh in her mind, she simply wanted confirmation that her father was indeed alive.

"Hey! I know," Kate said cheerily. "X rays don't take very long. The nurse has probably brought him back downstairs by now. Let's go and see, shall we?"

Sabrina sniffed and raised her head to look at Kate. "Okay," she said.

Lifting the child from the bed, Kate lowered her to the floor. When Sabrina's tiny hand slid into hers, Kate gave it a gentle squeeze. She led the way to the nurses' desk where Jackie stood talking on the phone.

As they approached, Jackie replaced the receiver. "Hi Kate. Who have we here?" she asked with a friendly smile.

"This is Sabrina. She's Dr. Diamond's daughter. Dr. Davis just checked her over, and she's fine. But she's worried about her father. Is he back from X ray?"

"Yes. I brought him down myself five minutes ago."

"Where is he? I thought he might like to see for himself that his daughter is all right."

"Uh…" Jackie began and darted a quick glance at the child who stood quietly at Kate's side. She leaned toward Kate. "He still hasn't regained consciousness," she whispered.

Kate felt Sabrina tug at her hand, and she bent to scoop the child into her arms.

"Can I see my daddy now?" Sabrina asked, anxiety threading her voice.

"I'm sorry, sweetie," Jackie quickly jumped in. "But it's against the rules."

Sabrina's eyes instantly filled with tears.

"I'll tell you what," Kate suggested, throwing Jackie a pleading glance. "If you stay here with Jackie, I'll go take a peek at your father and see how he is. Okay?"

Sabrina sniffed and nodded.

Moving around the desk, Kate settled Sabrina into the swivel chair.

"Dr. Franklin told me to put Dr. Diamond in the old plaster room down the hall. It's quieter and a little more private there," Jackie told Kate. "Heather's with him."

"Thanks." Kate turned to Sabrina. "I'll be right back."

Threading her way to the rear of Emerg, Kate paused at the door to the plaster room. Had Marsh regained consciousness? And if so, would he remember her?

Kate could still recall with vivid clarity the way he'd looked at her the night of the accident, an accident that nearly cost his sister, Piper, her life.

Piper Diamond, the popular, fun-loving and sometimes reckless sixteen-year-old, had been the only teenager at Kincade High who had made an effort to make Kate feel welcome, when Kate had transferred into the school in early March. Piper had taken her under her wing, instantly seeing through Kate's facade of careless indifference to the vulnerable, lonely girl beneath.

Once the high school had let out for the holidays, Kate had spent a lot of time with Piper and her brother, the handsome med student who'd come home to study for his exams. Marsh had even taught her how to ride, after first helping her overcome her childhood fear of horses.

Kate had enjoyed the fact that Piper and her brother had treated her like a member of the family, but as the hot summer days passed, her thoughts and feelings for Marsh had intensified and had been anything but sisterly, because she'd developed a giant-size crush on him. Only later had she seen that his friendship was nothing more than polite tolerance.

A bitter smile curled at the corners of her mouth

at the memory, a memory that still had the power to hurt. Annoyed at herself and the route her thoughts had taken, she drew a deep steadying breath and opened the door.

Heather Jones, also working part-time for the summer, glanced up from reading the patient's chart. "Kate, what brings you here?"

Kate darted a quick glance to the supine figure on the bed, noting his left arm wasn't in a cast but bandaged and in a sling, and proceeded to tell Heather about Sabrina's concern.

"He's rather restless," Heather said. "Dr. Franklin is confident it's only a matter of time before he'll regain consciousness. He was thrashing and moaning a few minutes ago, but he's settled down again."

Kate cast another nervous glance at the patient. "His arm isn't broken?"

"Apparently not. It's just a light sprain. He's a lucky man. The teenager who hit him wasn't wearing his seat belt, and his injuries are much worse. He had to have his spleen removed, not to mention that he's got a broken leg and multiple lacerations."

"That's too bad."

"Uh…Kate, I hate to ask, but while you're here, would you do me a favor?" Heather hurried on.

"A favor?"

"I'm under orders to stay with Dr. Diamond until he regains consciousness. But Dr. Franklin needs the lab results from a test he had done on another patient earlier tonight. Could you stick around while I run upstairs to the lab?"

Kate hesitated. "Sure," she finally said, certain Heather would do the same for her if the situation was reversed.

"Thanks. I'll be as quick as I can."

Kate stood for several seconds after Heather left, listening to the sound of Marsh's steady breathing. Slowly she inched her way toward him, her curiosity overriding her reluctance to be anywhere near the man who'd treated her with such disdain the last time they'd met. Her stomach muscles tightened with tension as her pulse kicked into high gear.

Slowly she studied his ashen face. He hadn't changed much. He looked older, more mature, but even after all this time he was still the most attractive man she'd ever known.

A clean dressing now covered the cut she'd treated earlier. His thick black hair, normally brushed back, was in careless disarray, falling across his forehead to soften his features. He looked totally vulnerable, completely defenseless, and Kate had to stop herself from reaching out to touch him. She felt her heart pound against her breastbone, then quickly right itself when she noticed that the bruise over his right eye had begun to change color, darkening from red to purple and spreading over his eyelids.

Continuing her perusal, Kate noted the sweeping curve of ebony lashes that were just like his daughter's, before her gaze settled on the fullness of his lips, lingering there for several long seconds.

Her pulse tripped in double time and a shiver chased through her as she recalled how she'd once tried to imagine what it would be like to have Marsh kiss her.

Suddenly his lips began to move, his mouth opening to emit a low, pain-filled moan.

Kate couldn't move. Her feet seemed to be glued to the floor as she watched his eyelids flicker before his lashes lifted to reveal incredible ice-blue eyes.

Marsh moaned again, louder this time, a sound that tore at Kate's heart. His arms started flailing, but the sling restricted his movements. He grew more frantic by the second, tugging at the bedclothes in an attempt to break free.

Fearful he might hurt himself, Kate placed her hands gently but firmly across his chest to restrain him.

Marsh's struggles intensified.

"Dr. Diamond. Please, take it easy." Kate spoke

softly, hoping to calm him. "You were in a car accident, and you've been brought to Mercy Hospital."

At her words he immediately stopped struggling. "An accident?" he repeated, his voice little more than a hoarse whisper. "My daughter? Where's my daughter? Is Sabrina all right?"

"Your daughter's fine," Kate assured him, wishing Heather would return, sure at any moment Marsh would turn and recognize her.

He clutched her arm, and she felt his fingers dig painfully into her flesh. "Why is it dark in here?" he asked, panic vibrating through his voice. "Why can't I see?"

Chapter Two

"This isn't happening!" Marsh said in a low growl of anger, frustration and pain.

Kate watched his handsome features contort. In an attempt to allay his fears, she covered his hand with hers, giving it a reassuring squeeze, ignoring the ripple of awareness that danced up her arm at the contact.

"Dr. Diamond, you're all right. Try to stay calm. You have several injuries, including a sprained left wrist. It's in a sling and restricting your movements."

"Where's Sabrina? I must find her," Marsh said, distress evident in his tone. Jerking his good hand free, he began to fumble with the bedcovers trying to push them aside.

"Dr. Diamond! Your daughter wasn't hurt in the accident. Trust me. She's quite safe," she added, but he was much too agitated to listen, shoving her unceremoniously aside, before sitting up and swinging his legs off the bed. But as soon as he stood a dizziness seemed to assail him, and his legs buckled beneath him.

Kate braced herself to take Marsh's weight. She managed to steady him, but the feel of his lean, muscular, near-naked body pressed hard against hers sent her pulse jumping around like a blip on a radar screen.

With every breath she drew, his earthy male scent swarmed her senses, transporting her back to the summer afternoon she'd slid off the back of a horse and right into his arms. Kate could still vividly recall those heart-stopping moments when he'd held her tight. They'd stared at each other for several long seconds, the air between them charged with tension.

"Marsh! What the hell do you think you're doing?" Dr. Franklin asked as he rushed in.

"Tom? Is that you?" Marsh asked tentatively. He broke free of Kate's grasp, turning his head in the direction of the new arrival.

"Yes, it's me. What are you doing out of bed? I take it you don't like your new role as patient?"

he commented as he and Heather approached the bed.

"You got that right."

"Why the frown? Are you having trouble with your eyesight?"

"It's nothing. I'll be fine in a minute. Someone forgot to turn on the lights, that's all," Marsh assured, but his voice sounded concerned.

"Nice try, Marsh. But the lights are on. I'd advise you to let the nurses help you back into bed so I can examine your eyes. And don't even think about arguing. You might be the hospital's new chief of staff, but your job doesn't start for another month. Besides, here in Emerg, I give the orders."

Kate glanced at Marsh and caught the look of frustration and resignation that flitted across his handsome features.

"Fine! Have it your way," Marsh said, sighing. "I'll extract my revenge on the racketball court," he added, in an obvious attempt to maintain some measure of control.

"It's a deal," Tom replied easily before nodding to Kate and Heather, who quickly moved to assist Marsh back into bed.

"Thanks, Kate," Heather whispered as they both left Dr. Franklin alone with his patient.

Outside in the hall Kate took a deep breath, willing her pulse, still racing, to slow down. Surely it wasn't possible after ten years, and especially after his unfair treatment of her then, that she was still attracted to Marshall Diamond?

Kate shook her head at the notion and then headed back to the nurses' desk, where Jackie stood comforting a woman who was weeping.

Behind them, exactly where Kate had left her, Sabrina sat, still hugging her stuffed teddy bear. When she caught sight of Kate, a look of relief came into her blue eyes.

"I'm sorry you had to wait so long." Kate crouched in front of the chair.

"Did you see my daddy?" Sabrina asked in an anxious voice.

"Yes, but only for a few minutes. I had to leave when the doctor came in."

"Is he all right?"

"Yes. But he has a cut on his forehead and a few nasty bruises," Kate answered truthfully. "He's probably going to have to stay in hospital overnight, just so the doctor can keep an eye on him," she went on, wanting to prepare Sabrina for that eventuality.

Kate chose not to mention Marsh's blindness, at least for now. Having seen similar injuries on other patients, she knew it was entirely probable his blindness was only temporary and would resolve itself in a few hours or by morning.

"Do I have to stay here, too?"

Kate smiled and shook her head. "By now the policeman who brought you in will have called your grandparents and told them about the accident. I bet they're on their way right now to pick you up and take you home."

"I don't want to go with them," Sabrina announced in a defiant voice, a scowl darkening her small features, a scowl Kate had seen before, one Sabrina had inherited from her father.

"Let's take a look in the waiting room and see if they've arrived, shall we?" Kate offered the child her hand.

Sabrina stared at Kate's outstretched hand for a long moment before reluctantly sliding off the chair. Tucking her teddy bear under one arm, she put her hand in Kate's.

As Kate led Sabrina out of the E.R., she silently acknowledged that she would be relieved to give Sabrina to her grandparents. It wasn't that she disliked the little girl, in fact the opposite was true. But this brief-but-unforgettable contact with the Diamond family had proven why she would need to keep her distance in the coming months.

Entering the busy waiting area, Kate immediately spotted the police officer. "I'm glad you're still here," she said as they approached him.

"Did the little one check out all right?"

"Yes. She's fine. Do you happen to know if her grandparents have arrived to take her home? They have been contacted about the accident, haven't they?"

"Well, not exactly, ma'am. I just talked to my sergeant, and he told me there's no one at the ranch. No one, that is, except the stable manager and the stable hands. Apparently the family flew to Ireland yesterday to attend a sale of Thoroughbred horses."

"Oh...I see," Kate replied. She knew the Blue Diamond Ranch was known around racing circles for its stable of winning Thoroughbreds.

Kate felt a gentle tug on her hand. She quickly crouched down to Sabrina's level.

"They're not coming, are they?" the child asked.

"No. But that's because—"

"I knew they wouldn't come." Sabrina continued in a voice that sounded cool and distant and much too grown-up for a five-year-old. "My mommy told me they didn't like me," she added.

"Oh, Sabrina! Surely not!" Kate reacted out of shock at the comment.

"Mommy said Daddy didn't like me, either," Sabrina blithely went on. "That's why he went away. But my mommy's dead, and I have to live with my daddy now."

"Oh, Sabrina! I'm sure your mother wouldn't have said such a thing about your father or your grandparents," Kate chided gently, astonished and dismayed by the child's comments.

"Yes, she did."

Kate didn't know how to respond. The little girl who'd been so anxious and concerned about her father earlier seemed to have vanished, and she couldn't understand why the change had occurred.

"My daddy's going to die, just like my mommy. Then I'll be all alone!" Burying her face in the bear's soft fur, she burst into tears.

Kate gently embraced Sabrina. "Oh, sweetie, don't cry," she crooned softly. "Your father isn't going to die. He's going to be fine. I promise," she added, lifting the weeping child into her arms.

"Should I contact Child Services?" the officer suggested.

Kate knew this was standard procedure when no family members were available to care for a child. But she was sure this would exact too high an emotional toll on the motherless child. Especially given the remarks Sabrina had made about her father and her grandparents.

During that summer ten years ago, when she and Piper had been friends, one of the things Kate had admired and envied about the Diamonds had been their strong family ties. She'd never forgotten the genuine warmth and love they'd had for one another. As Piper's friend, she'd had a taste of what this felt like. She'd even thought they'd accepted her. But Marsh had quickly set her straight.

"No, that's fine. I'll handle it," Kate quickly asserted, as Sabrina's grip on her tightened.

Kate readily acknowledged she was being over-protective and that Sabrina's welfare was really none of her business. But she remembered how frightening it had been once when she'd been placed in a foster home for a few days with strangers, well-meaning people who'd tried to be kind, tried to understand.

She'd been so terrified she wouldn't see her father again, she'd learned to accept his drinking without complaint. He was all she had left of family, and she'd been determined to stay with him whatever the cost.

"Marsh, be reasonable. How can I release you tonight? Not only are you suffering from a concussion, a mild one I grant you, but you can't see—" Tom Franklin broke off and let out a sigh. Closing his patient's chart, he moved to stand next to the bed.

"You're a damned good doctor, Marsh, one of the best, and I agree with your diagnosis, that your blindness is more than likely only temporary—"

"Then let me out of here. Let me go home," Marsh quickly cut in, though he suspected from the tone of Tom's voice the argument was already lost.

"You always were a stubborn son of a gun," Tom remarked. "But I can't, in good conscience, allow you to leave," he went on. "Believe me, if the situations were reversed, you'd be reading me the riot act for even suggesting it.

"You know as well as I do, even if the swelling behind your eyes goes down and the pressure on the optic nerves is removed, your vision won't necessarily return right away. You're going to have to bite the bullet and spend the night. We'll reassess your condition in the morning."

"All right!" Marsh grunted. Much as he liked and respected his colleague, Tom's voice was beginning to grate on him, compounding the headache still throbbing at his temples, the same headache he'd only minutes ago denied even existed.

"You concede? Well, this is a first," Tom responded with a soft chuckle.

"I don't have much choice, do I?" Marsh countered, suddenly drained. "But what about my daughter? Are you sure she's all right?"

"I was in Emerg when you and the other driver were brought in, but I didn't see your daughter. No doubt by now the police will have contacted your folks, and they'll be on their way to the hospital. But, if it will stop you worrying, I'll see what I can find out about your little girl."

"Thanks. I just hope my folks are home," he added on a sigh. "They didn't know we were coming today. I wanted to surprise them."

"I know they've been looking forward to your return. What about Piper? Is she home, or is she still in Europe working for that magazine?"

"She's still in Europe," Marsh responded, thinking it had been five years since he'd last seen his baby sister.

"Well, I'm sure we can figure out something. I'll see what I can find out," Tom said. "In the meantime I've arranged to move you upstairs to a private room."

Marsh felt Tom's hand on his shoulder. "Relax and try not to worry."

"Easy for you to say," Marsh mumbled under his breath. He listened to the sound of his colleague's footsteps cross the floor, followed moments later by the hiss of the door as it closed.

A heavy silence descended, and instantly a feeling of panic started to build inside him like a summer squall. The darkness seemed to press down, entombing him, bringing home the stark and inescapable reality that he was blind.

Where there once had been light and colors,

depth and delineation, people and movement, now there was only an all-encompassing blackness that seemed to devour him, thrusting him unwillingly into the role of prisoner.

His breath hitched and locked in his throat, causing his heart to beat against his ribs at an alarming rate. Pain pounded inside his head, and the sour taste of bile rose in his throat. Swallowing repeatedly, he fought down the nausea making him gag.

Angry at his body's show of weakness, a weakness he couldn't seem to overcome, he gripped the bedsheet with his right hand. He braced himself as another wave of panic slammed into him, sending his heart rate accelerating once more.

Muttering a litany of curses, Marsh concentrated on slowly and deliberately filling his lungs with oxygen, before releasing it in one long, cleansing breath. He repeated the action, only this time, mingled in with the hospital smell of antiseptic, Marsh caught the delicate and exotic scent of jasmine.

Momentarily distracted, he frowned. The scent was vaguely familiar, but he couldn't for the life of him think why. A memory danced on the edges of his mind, just out of reach. He inhaled again, hoping to recapture the perfume and perhaps jog the memory free, but the scent was no longer detectable.

It had to have come from one of the nurses, he

silently reasoned, probably the one who'd tried to stop him getting out of bed, the one who'd prevented him from falling.

He remembered leaning hard against her for support, feeling her strength as well as her softness, recalled how there had indeed been the scent of jasmine in the air.

He shook his head. Undoubtedly his sense of smell was heightened by his blindness.

Marsh gradually loosened his grip on the bedcovers and, wanting to keep the panic at bay, turned his thoughts to the accident.

The last thing he remembered was seeing the flashing amber lights, warning them they were approaching Cutter's Junction, a busy intersection to the south of Kincade. He'd been talking to Sabrina, telling her how much they were going to enjoy living at the Blue Diamond Ranch with her grandparents and her uncle Spencer.

But the happy homecoming he'd envisaged had taken a bad turn, and now he found himself trapped in a world of darkness. Nothing in his thirty-seven years had prepared him for this new and alien world, a world without vision, a world that left him feeling totally powerless and utterly defenseless. Was this his punishment for turning his back on his daughter?

Chapter Three

"**K**ate, why don't you take Sabrina upstairs to see her father?"

Kate opened her mouth to object, then shut it again, knowing she should have anticipated Dr. Franklin's request. After she'd found him and explained the situation, Sabrina had begged to see her daddy.

"Is there a problem? I have a few charts to write up before I finish here."

"No," Kate replied, darting a quick glance at Sabrina. "It's just...well, I mean..." She floundered. "Is he able to—?" She ground to a halt, hoping Dr. Franklin would be astute enough to fill in the blank himself.

"Oh—right." Dr. Franklin nodded in understanding. He turned to the child. "There is something you should know. When the accident happened your father got a rather nasty cut on his forehead as well as a few bruises and a black eye."

"A black eye?" Sabrina repeated. "I've never seen a black eye before."

"Oh…and that's not all," the doctor continued in the same light vein. "Because of the bump to his head and the bruising around his eyes, your father isn't able to see."

Sabrina threw Kate a worried look before turning back to the doctor.

"I know that sounds scary," Dr. Franklin continued evenly. "And believe me, your father isn't happy about it, either," he added in an attempt to make Sabrina smile. "But once the swelling goes down, he'll be just fine."

"He'll see again?"

"He'll see again," the doctor acknowledged.

The news of her father's condition didn't appear to have upset the little girl unduly, and silently Kate credited the calm, matter-of-fact way Dr. Franklin had explained the situation.

"Can I see him now?"

"Yes. He's upstairs in Room 516," he told Kate. "I'll catch up with you in a few minutes."

Kate carried Sabrina to the elevators and lowered her to the floor after pressing the call button. "Dr. Franklin's nice, isn't he?"

"Can I press the number?" Sabrina asked as she scampered inside the elevator that had just arrived.

"Sure," Kate replied, pleased that the prospect of seeing her father had cheered Sabrina. She herself had mixed feelings on the matter.

When they got out on the fifth floor, Kate felt Sabrina's hand slip into hers and glancing down at the child, she flashed her a smile. "Everything's going to be just fine." But she saw that Sabrina's steps had already slowed, and a look of apprehension clouded her small features. Kate gave Sabrina's hand a squeeze. After tapping the door lightly, she pushed it open.

"Who's there?" Marsh asked, annoyed to hear a slight tremor in his voice. Since the nurse named Heather had left, he'd become restless and agitated, hating the continuous darkness.

"Dr. Diamond. I'm the nurse who tended you earlier. I've brought your daughter to see you." She tugged gently at Sabrina, who was standing behind Kate clutching her teddy.

"Sabrina? Sweetheart, are you all right?" Relief and excitement echoed in Marsh's voice. He'd been fighting the urge to get up and go in search of Sabrina, foolish as he'd known it would be. But he'd needed to hear her voice, to know she was indeed all right.

Sabrina made no reply.

"Say hello to your father, Sabrina." The nurse gently coaxed the child.

"Hello, Daddy."

"Are you all right? Are they taking care of you?" he asked, trying with difficulty to keep his tone even, so as not to frighten her.

Silence followed his questions, and he had to bite back his frustration at her nonresponse. During the past four months, ever since he'd brought her home, she'd driven him to distraction at times by her unwillingness to communicate. He wished he could see her, see for himself that she was unhurt.

"She's fine. Not so much as a scratch," the nurse told him.

Behind them the door opened, and Dr. Franklin entered.

"The doctor man said you can't see," Sabrina suddenly announced, her natural curiosity winning the battle with her reserve.

Marsh's mouth curved into a semblance of a smile. "If you mean Dr. Franklin, then he's right."

"I'll take that as a compliment," Dr. Franklin said.

"Tom? Where did you come from? I didn't know you were there." But there was relief in

Marsh's tone at the presence of his friend. "I was telling Sabrina you were right about me not being able to see," Marsh went on, attempting to make light of the situation.

"It's only a temporary setback," Tom said easily.

"Sabrina, why don't you climb up here beside me?" Marsh suggested, patting the covers with his uninjured hand. Hearing his daughter's voice had reassured him somewhat, but he had a longing to touch her.

"Kate can lift you onto the bed," said Dr. Franklin.

"Kate?" Marsh repeated the name, and at the sound of it Kate felt her pulse wobble.

"Kate's nice. She's the nurse who's been looking after me."

"And me, too, I believe. Thank you, Kate, for all you've done."

"You're welcome," she murmured, lifting Sabrina onto the bed.

Marsh felt the movement beside him, and instinctively he reached out to her. His hand made contact with warm, bare skin, and for a split second he felt a tiny jolt of electricity zip up his arm.

The air suddenly seemed rife with tension, a tension he didn't understand. Puzzled, he curled his fingers around what he guessed was a forearm, but he knew by its size it didn't belong to Sabrina.

Marsh heard a sharp intake of breath at the same time as the scent of jasmine assailed him. He instantly recognized it as being the fragrance he'd found strangely disturbing earlier. Once again a memory danced elusively at the edges of his mind, only to drift out of reach.

"Daddy that's Kate's arm." Sabrina's childish giggle effectively distracted Marsh, and he released his hold on Kate.

"Sorry."

"That's all right," Kate responded, her voice a throaty whisper. She backed away, ignoring the tingle of pleasure his touch evoked, telling her all too clearly that even now he still affected her as no other man ever had.

"By the way, Marsh. I don't know if Kate has had time to mention it, but your parents aren't at the ranch. They're out of the country."

"What about Spencer? Surely he's around?" Marsh had talked to his mother a few weeks ago, confirming their arrival at the end of August. He'd managed to wind things up two weeks early and so had decided to surprise them.

"Afraid not. Apparently they've all gone to Ireland."

"Ireland! Oh! Right. Spencer did mention something about the annual Thoroughbred sales. I didn't realize my folks planned to go with him.''

''Unfortunately that's going to complicate matters.''

''What do you mean?''

''Arrangements need to be made for Sabrina's care, at least until your eyesight returns.''

''Hold on a minute.'' Marsh tried to stay calm. ''What kind of arrangements?'' He reached out rather awkwardly in search of Sabrina and felt his fingers brush her hair.

''I'd offer to take Sabrina home with me,'' Tom said, ''but Amy, my four-year-old, has the chicken pox. I'm afraid we're running out of options.''

''What about Mrs. B., the housekeeper?'' Kate jumped in, recalling the older woman who'd worked for the Diamond family for a number of years.

Marsh slowly shook his head. ''Mrs. B. retired earlier this year and moved to Arizona to live with her brother,'' he explained.

''She wasn't replaced?'' Tom asked.

''No. My father's taken over the kitchen. He likes to cook,'' Marsh explained. ''I was planning on putting an ad in the paper next week for a part-time sitter.''

''I'm afraid that leaves us with no choice,'' Tom said.

"Wait," Marsh said, knowing what Tom was referring to, but unwilling to let anyone hand his daughter over to Child Services. The upheavals she'd faced lately were quite enough for any five-year-old to be coping with. What Sabrina needed was stability.

"Tom—" Marsh began, as his mind scrambled to come up with another solution. "We both agree that my, uh, injuries, that is my, uh, eyesight will probably be restored by morning, and I'll be able to go home," he said in a positive manner. "Perhaps Sabrina could spend the night at the hospital? What do you think, Sabrina? You wouldn't mind staying here would you?"

"Where would I sleep?"

"I'm sure Dr. Franklin could scrounge up a spare bed for you and let you sleep in here with me," Marsh replied, pleased Sabrina hadn't immediately rejected the prospect of spending the night at the hospital.

"Hold on a second," Tom cautioned.

"Aw…come on, Tom! It isn't too much to ask, is it?" Marsh cajoled softly. "And if you're worried about hospital policy, you could always admit Sabrina overnight for observation. She was in a car accident, remember?"

Kate had watched the interchange with interest. She could have bitten her tongue when she mentioned the housekeeper, thinking for a moment Marsh might ask how she knew about Mrs. B., but he hadn't appeared to notice.

She knew by the continuing silence that Dr. Franklin's resolve was weakening. Marsh had offered a viable solution.

"I think that could be arranged. Kate, see if you can hustle up another bed and haul it in here. I'll take care of the paperwork."

"Yes, Doctor," she replied and quickly withdrew.

Moments later, with the help of an orderly, Kate maneuvered another hospital bed into the private room. Dr. Franklin had already left.

"Kate?" Marsh began tentatively. "You don't mind if I call you Kate, do you?"

"Of course, not," she answered as she shook out a crisp, clean, hospital sheet.

"What time is it?"

"Nine-thirty. Why?"

"Sabrina was just saying she's hungry. Is there any way you could get her something to eat?"

"Sure. After I finish making up the bed, I'll pop down to the cafeteria and see what I can find. Would a peanut butter sandwich and a glass of milk be all right?" she asked as she deftly tucked in the sheet.

"Yes, please," Sabrina was quick to reply. "Can I eat it in bed?"

"Sure," Kate replied picking up a pillow and slipping on its cover.

"Mommy had rules. She never let me eat in bed."

"Here in Kincade the rules are different," Marsh countered lightly. "Isn't that right, Kate?" he added with a hint of humor.

Kate felt her pulse skip a beat at the casual-but-friendly way he included her in the conversation.

"That's right," she agreed, smoothing out the blanket, glad he couldn't see the blush creeping into her cheeks. "In fact, it's a rule here at Mercy Hospital that you must eat in bed," she added, and at the sound of Marsh's soft chuckle a shiver chased down her spine.

"Wow! For sure?" Sabrina asked, obviously unsure whether or not Kate was teasing her.

"For sure," Kate said with a smile.

"How long have you been a nurse, Kate?" Marsh suddenly asked.

"Seven years."

"Have you worked at Mercy all that time?"

"No. I'm only filling in for nurses taking their summer vacations. My last shift is tomorrow morning, then I'll be looking for another job to tide me over until the new wing opens in September."

"You'll be working in the new wing?"

"Yes," Kate replied, not altogether sure why she was telling Marsh. "If you'll excuse me," she went on, "I'll pop down to the cafeteria now, it closes at ten," she said. "Would you like me to bring you something, too?"

"No, but thanks."

"I'll be right back." Kate flashed Sabrina a smile before slipping out of the room.

The cafeteria, downstairs on the third floor, was almost deserted. Kate asked one of the kitchen workers for a peanut butter sandwich and while she waited, she remembered why she'd wanted to return to Kincade after her divorce.

Kincade hadn't been the first place she and her father had moved to that year, and Kate had known from experience that it wouldn't be the last. Her father rarely managed to keep a job for more than a couple of months, usually getting fired either for fighting or drinking, or both.

As it was they'd stayed seven months, twice as long as in most places. For the first time in her life Kate had not only felt at home, she'd made a friend.

Piper Diamond's easy acceptance of her had been the one bright light in what had been a life of constant change, a life of struggle, a life of misery. Unlike some folks, Piper hadn't judged Kate by her appearance or by the amount of money she'd had, she'd simply accepted her for herself. For a little while, Kate had tasted happiness. She'd even foolishly begun to hope that maybe this time they would put down roots, this time they would make a real home.

She should have known it wouldn't last. And on the morning after Piper's accident, her father had told her to pack her bags, they were moving on. Once again he'd been fired for drinking on the job.

They'd driven through Arizona and New Mexico, ending up in Texas, where her father had found a part-time job on a cattle ranch. By then, she'd applied for entry into a training program for nurses. Just before graduation, she'd received a letter of acceptance.

Her father's job had ended and once again he'd told her they were moving. But this time Kate, old enough to fend for herself and wanting to strive for her own dream, refused to go with him.

After successfully completing her training she'd moved to Los Angeles. While working at a hospital there, she'd met and married Dan Turner. But she'd never forgotten those months she'd spent in Kincade.

Ever since her mother's death, she'd dreamed of belonging. And Kincade had once embodied that dream.

When she spotted the ad for nurses to staff Kincade Mercy Hospital's new wing, she'd leaped at the chance to come back.

She'd known for several years that Dr. Marshall Diamond worked in Chicago, so she'd felt reasonably sure the chances of running into him again were slim. The risk had seemed worth it.

"Here's your peanut butter sandwich." The voice cut through Kate's meandering thoughts.

"Thanks," Kate said and carried the tray to the cashier. Back upstairs she tapped lightly on the door, before entering.

"It's only me," she said, then came to a halt when she saw Sabrina lying across Marsh's legs, fast asleep.

"She fell asleep," Marsh said in a hushed voice. "At least I think she's asleep. She hasn't made a move in the past five minutes."

"She's asleep, all right," Kate confirmed as she crossed to set the tray on the table at the foot of Marsh's bed. "I'll put her to bed, shall I?"

"I think we'll both be more comfortable if you do."

Kate carefully lifted Sabrina from her father's bed and carried her to the one she'd made up nearby. Lowering the sleeping child onto the blankets, Kate carefully removed Sabrina's shoes, socks and shorts, leaving only her T-shirt and underwear.

"She's had quite a day," Marsh said.

"You both have. You should try to get some sleep, too, Dr. Diamond," she added as she eased Sabrina between the sheets.

After pulling the covers over Sabrina, Kate approached Marsh's bed. She unhooked the call button from the wall behind him. "If you need anything during the night just press the call button," she told him as she placed it in his uninjured hand.

Kate started to withdraw, but Marsh quickly curled his fingers around her hand to stop her.

"Thank you, for all you've done for Sabrina tonight."

Kate couldn't speak. Tiny rivulets of sensation were traveling up her arm, causing her breath to catch in her throat and her pulse to stumble drunkenly. It was all she could do not to pull free.

Although she'd often imagined what she would say or do if she ever ran into Marshall Diamond again, none of the scenarios she'd envisioned had come anywhere near the real thing.

"I'm just doing my job. Goodnight, Dr. Diamond," she managed to say, before slipping from the room.

"There's no change?" Dr. Franklin asked, after he'd completed his examination of Marsh's eyes the next morning.

"No change," Marsh confirmed in a tight voice. "What about the scan you did earlier this morning? Have you got the results back yet?"

"Everything appears normal. There's certainly nothing to indicate the damage is in any way permanent. And remember, Marsh, it hasn't been twenty-four hours since the accident."

Marsh sighed. The results of the scan were reassuring, but it brought only a small measure of comfort. Anxiety and the irrational fear that his sight might never return had kept him awake for most of the night.

At odd times he'd opened his eyes, silently sending up a prayer for some small sign—a blurry image, a shadowy shape, some indication that his vision was returning. The blackness remained.

Lying in the stillness and silence, Marsh had listened to the sounds of his daughter breathing nearby, deeply grateful she'd come through the accident unscathed.

"Come on, buddy," Tom said. "I did warn you, you were being optimistic in thinking your sight would be back to normal by this morning."

"But I can't stay here another day."

"You don't have much choice in the matter. Where's Sabrina? Did she sleep all right?"

"She slept like a top. I asked one of the nurses to give her a bath."

"I'm afraid I'm going to have to make a call to Child Services."

"Damn it, Tom! Is that really necessary?" Marsh asked, anger vibrating through him.

"Marsh, I sympathize, truly I do. You know I'd take her home with me, but I doubt you want to add chicken pox to your list of problems. Why don't you call your mother in Ireland and ask her to come back?"

"Because by the time she gets here my eyesight will probably have returned, and she'll have made the journey for nothing."

"What about a neighbor?"

"I've been away so long I don't know any of the neighbors anymore..."

"Then we've run out of options...unless—"

"Unless what?" Marsh instantly responded. "What?" he repeated, trying to keep his frustration under wraps.

"Well, I'm not sure it's really any different than foster care, but I suppose you could hire someone to look after Sabrina for a few days, until your sight returns," Tom said.

Marsh was silent for a moment, pondering his friend's suggestion. Suddenly a thought struck him. "Why don't I hire a nurse to look after both

of us? Would that be enough to get you to sign my
release papers and let me go home with my daughter?''

"That wasn't what I had in mind—''

"Maybe not, but it's what I have in mind.''

"It's a viable alternative,'' Tom acknowledged.
"But how do you expect to find someone on such
short notice?''

Marsh was quiet for a moment, his thoughts racing. Surely he could find a nurse...

"Wait a minute! What about Kate? The nurse
Sabrina liked, the one who brought her up here last
night?'' Marsh asked.

"Kate Turner?'' Tom said. "How do you know
she's available?''

"Because last night she told me she only had
one more shift to work, and that was this morning.
Maybe she'd be interested working for me for a
day, two at the most,'' he went on, excitement bubbling in his voice. "She'd be perfect. Sabrina already knows and likes her...''

"It certainly wouldn't do any harm to ask,''
Tom said.

"Do me a favor, Tom. Find Kate and ask her to
come and see me?''

A few minutes later Dr. Franklin reappeared
with Kate.

"Kate? Last night you told me that when you

finished your shift today you'd be looking for another job,'' Marsh said.

''Yes, that's right,'' Kate replied sounding puzzled.

''Would you like to come and work for me?''

•

Chapter Four

"**Y**ou want to offer me a job?" Kate stared at Marsh unable to believe what she'd just heard.

"It's only for a day or two. And you did say yesterday you'd be out of a job when your shift ended today, didn't you?"

"Yes, but—"

"I want to take my daughter home. And Dr. Franklin has assured me that if I find someone willing to take on the job of looking after both Sabrina and me until my sight returns, he'd release me from the hospital today," Marsh cut in. "Right, Tom?"

"Yes," Tom Franklin acknowledged.

"So, Kate...I'd very much appreciate it if you

could see your way to helping us out.'' Marsh's tone was warm and persuasive. ''I'll pay you well for your time,'' he added, quoting an hourly rate that made Kate blink.

''That's very generous, but...''

''Please, I'm desperate.'' He jumped in before she could finish. ''I'm not asking for myself. I'm asking for my daughter. It's the only alternative. I really don't think Sabrina could handle being in foster care, not after all she's been through lately.''

Kate heard his underlying cry for help, and she could see the anxiety etched on his bruised features. Still she hesitated. Ten years ago he'd treated her badly and broken her heart in the process. Though she'd grown up and changed since then, the pain lingered and she was reluctant to let herself become involved in his life again. She knew she should tell Marsh she couldn't work for him for any price, but the words stuck in her throat.

''I appreciate your position—'' Kate finally began, but before she could continue the door behind her opened and Sabrina, dressed once more in her shorts and T-shirt, appeared with one of the nurses.

''Hi, Kate!'' Sabrina flashed a shy smile.

''Hello, Sabrina,'' Kate replied, warmed by the child's friendly greeting.

''Are we going home now, Daddy?'' Sabrina asked as she approached her father's bed.

"I hope so. I'm waiting for Kate."

Sabrina darted a quick glance at her. "Is she coming, too?" she asked, expectancy and hope in her blue eyes, and for the life of her, Kate couldn't find it in her heart to say no.

"Yes, I'm coming, too," Kate said after a brief pause, and caught the look of relief that softened the lines of worry on Marsh's face.

"Yeah!" Sabrina said, then grinned.

"Thank you, Kate. You won't regret it," Marsh said.

Kate flashed Sabrina a smile, telling herself she was only agreeing to take on the job for the little girl's sake, and hoping all the while she wasn't making the biggest mistake of her life.

Kate still couldn't believe she'd actually agreed to work for him. If anyone had told her two days ago she'd be accompanying Marsh Diamond and his daughter to the Blue Diamond Ranch to work as a private nurse, she would have laughed in their faces.

Dr. Franklin had been as good as his word, signing Marsh's release without fanfare, telling him to return to the hospital for a follow-up examination when any change occurred. Marsh had immediately asked for his clothes and proceeded to issue instructions, including suggesting Kate go home and pack a few things, enough for two or three days.

Her shift over, she'd done exactly that, returning to the small motel room she'd been renting on a weekly basis since she'd arrived. She'd planned to hunt for a small furnished apartment close to the hospital, but that would have to wait until she had a few paychecks under her belt.

As she drove past the white picket fence leading to the front of the ranch house, Kate was suddenly struck with a feeling of coming home. She told herself it was ridiculous. But as she gazed at the familiar, sprawling ranch house, with its wide wooden veranda alive with hanging baskets of pink and red geraniums and trailing lobelia, she was surprised that the place still touched a chord somewhere deep inside her.

After she brought the car to a halt on the graveled driveway, Marsh turned his head in a stiff jerky motion as though listening for something. "Are we home?"

Kate felt her heart shudder to a halt at the question. "Yes," she replied, her voice void of expression.

Reaching for the door handle, she quickly climbed out. She turned to offer her assistance, but he was already sliding across the seat patting the air with his right hand in search of the door frame.

She opened the other door for Sabrina, who hopped out to gaze up at the house that was to be her new home. Sabrina was already scampering up the stairs when Kate returned to Marsh's side.

Marsh stumbled on the loose gravel, and Kate quickly steadied him, ignoring the jolt that traveled up her arm at the contact. His grip on her arm was viselike, and she could feel the tension and frustration coming off him in waves.

"It will be easier if you let me lead you." Taking his right hand she tucked it in the crook of her arm. "The stairs to the veranda are approximately twenty yards directly ahead of us."

Marsh nodded, and when she moved off, he followed a half step behind her.

"How do we get inside if there's nobody here?" Sabrina asked once they'd safely negotiated the stairs.

"I called earlier and told the stable manager we'd be coming home today," Marsh said. "He told me he'd open up the house for us, and he also said our suitcases and everything from the car had been delivered by a patrolman this morning."

"Is my turtle backpack with my toys and books here too?"

"I should think so."

"Sabrina, why don't you open the front door for your father?"

After she'd carefully eased Marsh through the doorway, Kate felt her heart skip a beat at finding herself once again inside the Diamond home. This was the one place she'd never thought she would ever set foot in again.

For a brief moment she indulged in the fantasy that this was her home, her husband, her child. How many times had she dreamed this scenario that summer ten years ago? But that was before Marsh had turned on her, believing she was responsible for his sister's near drowning.

She'd spent her childhood wishing and hoping for things that never came true. If her mother hadn't died, everything would have been different. Her father wouldn't have started drinking, they wouldn't have had to keep moving every few months from place to place, they could have stayed in one place, put down roots and had a real home and family.

Kate hadn't seen her father for three years, but she knew he was probably sitting in a bar somewhere. From an early age she'd had to live with the shame of being the child of an alcoholic parent. She'd grown to hate the disapproving and often pitying looks thrown her way. And she'd had to develop a thick skin and a belligerent attitude, just so she could handle the jibes and taunts tossed at her by cruel and insensitive kids. She'd pretended not to care. Love was just another four-letter word, and the only person she could count on was herself.

Her marriage had certainly proven that. When she met Dan Turner, she was working as a nurse in Los Angeles. Dan had been badly injured in an accident on a construction site and he'd ended up in hospital for more than five months. During that time he'd undergone several operations and each time he'd awakened from the anesthetic, Kate had been at his bedside. She'd admired his courage in the face of his injuries.

They'd become friends; a friendship that had deepened into what they both believed was love. On the day of his release from hospital he'd asked her to marry him. Impulsively, foolishly, she'd said yes.

It hadn't taken long to realize they'd made a mistake. Dan had confused gratitude for her support for love, while Kate had confused friendship for love, hoping it would be enough on which to build a dream.

They'd stayed together for almost a year, until Dan completed his rehabilitation. He'd moved out shortly afterward, and they'd remained friends— even after she filed for divorce.

"Where's my room?" Sabrina asked, cutting through Kate's wayward thoughts.

"Upstairs," Marsh replied. "I bet your grandmother has a room all ready for you."

"Really?" Sabrina asked, her blue eyes alight with excitement.

"Kate," he angled his body toward her. "If you take me to the living room on the right, and find me an easy chair, you and Sabrina can go upstairs and explore the bedrooms.

"My parents' bedroom is down here on the main floor. Once you've figured out which room is Sabrina's and which room is mine, feel free to choose another for yourself."

"Why don't you come with us?" Kate suggested, feeling strongly that he should be the one to take Sabrina upstairs.

"Thanks, but I'll pass," he said, an edge to his voice. "Being led around is not exactly my idea of fun."

"I'm sorry," Kate said softly, easily understanding his frustration and his anger. This was his first venture into the unknown world of total darkness, and all things considered, he'd managed exceedingly well.

She did as he asked and led him into the living room, maneuvering him past a small plant table and around a lamp. Stopping in front of the easy chair, she took his hand and placed it on the arm of the chair and waited until he lowered himself into it.

A quick glance around told Kate everything seemed much the same as before. The room was big and bright with sunlight streaking in through the bay window overlooking the veranda. There was a quiet and inescapable elegance about the room Kate had never forgotten.

"We won't be long," she told him once he was settled.

"Don't rush on my account. I'll be fine," Marsh drawled as he relaxed against the cushions, but Kate wasn't taken in by his nonchalance, seeing the tension in the taut line of his jaw. The temptation to offer words of comfort was strong, but she quashed it, feeling sure Marsh would regard any show of concern for him as pity. He was a proud man, a man accustomed to being in complete control. That he found his blindness irritating was an understatement, and Kate could only hope for his sake his sight would return soon.

Marsh listened as Kate and Sabrina's footsteps and voices faded away. Ironically he found himself wishing he was back at the hospital where life had seemed infinitely simpler. But then he hadn't expected to feel quite so helpless or so completely powerless.

He curled his hands into two tight fists, then

cursed softly at the pain that shot up his sprained wrist. The urge to hit something, to scream and yell, almost overwhelmed him. Instead he focused on breathing deeply, and slowly his hands relaxed until the pain subsided.

Beneath his open palms, he could feel the smooth fabric of the armchair. He knew he was sitting in his mother's favorite chair, a cream-colored, brocade easy chair near the bay window, where she loved to sit and work on her cross-stitch.

Though he hadn't been home in more than three years, he could easily conjure up in his mind exactly how the room looked. Across from him would be two matching love seats angled to face the granite fireplace, and behind him and to the right, against the inside wall, was a mahogany sideboard and two tall antique bookcases filled with the leather-bound editions his father loved to collect.

Suddenly he realized just how much he'd missed this, his childhood home, as well as his family. When he'd married Tiffany six years ago, he'd felt sure theirs would be a solid marriage, like the one his parents had enjoyed for the past forty years. He'd believed his beautiful, sophisticated bride had wanted the same things, a home, a family and a loving and equal partnership.

Marsh let out a sigh, wondering, not for the first

time, how he could have been such a fool. He ground his teeth together as the old anger surfaced once more. Two years ago his world had come crumbling down when he'd discovered his wife in bed with another man. Tiffany had tried to tell him it was all a mistake, he hadn't really seen what he'd seen. He'd laughed at her audacity, and she'd been enraged by his reaction, declaring everyone had affairs, that he should simply accept it and not make a fuss.

He'd moved out of the house and headed straight for a divorce lawyer. At night, unable to sleep, he'd been plagued with the notion that perhaps he'd been at fault, that his dedication to his career had been the reason for Tiffany's betrayal. He'd even begun to doubt he was cut out to be a father or a husband.

Too late he'd realized he wasn't the only one who'd suffered in the breakup of his marriage. Sabrina had been an innocent bystander.

When he'd tried to remedy the situation by filing for joint custody, Tiffany had turned nasty and revengeful.

His wife's sudden death in a boating accident had thrust him into the role of full-time parent, and he'd quickly realized he hadn't a clue as to the needs of a five-year-old—a child, he was ashamed to admit, he hardly knew.

He'd hoped that by coming home to the California countryside, to the ranch where he'd spent his own happy and fun-filled childhood with his parents and his brother and sister, he could perhaps in time break down the barriers his daughter had built around her heart. Barriers his absence had helped forge. Barriers that had no doubt been fortified by his bitter and vengeful ex-wife.

The sound of voices cut through his meanderings, and as he listened to Kate and Sabrina approaching, he found himself fervently wishing his sight would return. Only then would he be in full control.

"Daddy, we found my room," Sabrina said excitedly as she ran ahead of Kate into the living room. "It's nice. I really like—"

"Good," Marsh jumped in, interrupting Sabrina. "Kate are you there?"

"Yes, I'm right here. Is anything wrong?"

"I have a headache," he said gruffly as he rose awkwardly from the chair. "I'd like to go upstairs and lie down."

"Of course." Kate quickly moved to his side. Taking his right hand she tucked it once again at her elbow. "Sabrina, why don't you run on ahead and count how many stairs there are up to the landing," she suggested, wanting to erase the look of disappointment from the child's face. "Dr. Diamond, I know this is trying for you—"

"It's Marsh. And if you're planning on giving me a lecture, don't."

"Fine," Kate responded curtly, tempted for a moment to free his hand and let him fend for himself. She corralled her anger and, moving slowly, led him out of the living room into the foyer.

Sabrina was already at the top of the stairs.

"There's ten steps and then four more," Sabrina called down from the top of the stairs.

"Thank you, Sabrina," Kate responded.

"Can I go to my room and play?"

"Of course."

Kate approached the stairs and stopped. "Bottom step," she said as Marsh located it with his shoe before starting to climb.

"The room your mother prepared for Sabrina is lovely," Kate said once they'd successfully reached the upper landing.

"My room is the second on the right," Marsh said, ignoring her comment.

"I know...uh, I mean, I know this must feel really strange," Kate stammered. Feeling her face grow warm, she wondered if he noticed her slip.

"It's no picnic. It would help if I could get some indication that my sight was returning."

"Give it time," Kate said softly, slowing to a halt.

She reached for his door handle, noticing as she did that her heart rate had begun to accelerate. Glancing into the room, she saw several potential hazards in the form of scatter mats on the hard-wood floor.

"Wait right here for a minute," she instructed, moving his hand to the door frame. "I need to move a few things to reduce your chances of tripping, slipping or falling."

Entering Marsh's bedroom, she gathered up the scatter mats, sliding them under the bed, then pushed a chair and a floor lamp out of harm's way.

She stood for a moment studying the room, a room she'd glanced into a number of times that long-ago summer. It didn't appear to have changed. Decorated in earth shades, it was a mas-culine room with only a few splashes of color sup-plied by the pillows on the bed and several bright paintings on the walls.

"Are you finished?" Marsh's voice held an edge of impatience, and Kate quickly returned to his side.

"That should do it. You'll be able to practice in here with your cane."

She watched his mouth twist into a thin line. "I

don't plan on practicing anything with it," he said as she led him inside.

"You'll find it very useful," Kate said, surprised and a little annoyed at his dismissal of the cane. "You should also think about counting the number of steps it takes you to get to different points in the room—"

"I'd like to rest now."

Kate bit back a sigh. While she understood his reluctance to adapt to his blindness, especially when his condition was only temporary, his attitude surprised her.

He'd always been so upbeat and fun, as well as patient and understanding. She felt sure that if he tried to master the situation, rather than become a prisoner of it, not only would it distract him but it would also help fill the hours until his sight returned.

"Can I bring you an aspirin and some water?"

"No, thanks. Did you find a suitable room for yourself?"

"I chose the room down the hall on the left," she told him as she stopped near the foot of Marsh's bed. Taking his hand she placed it on the bedpost.

"That's my sister's room."

"If it's a problem I can choose another," Kate

said, refraining from adding that she'd known it was Piper's room, that's why she'd chosen it.

"It's not a problem. She's in Europe. At least she was the last time I heard from her. She travels around a lot."

"What does Piper do for a living?" Kate asked, keeping her tone casual, but curious to know what her friend had settled on for her chosen career.

Marsh frowned. "Uh…she's a freelance photographer," he replied after a brief hesitation.

"Sounds exciting!" Kate commented, not at all surprised by the news. Even as a teen Piper had had a flair for taking pictures. She'd carried a camera around her neck constantly, enabling her to snap pictures of anything that caught her fancy. Piper had also enjoyed developing the black-and-white pictures herself, and had done so in the darkroom her father had built her off the kitchen. Kate had spent hours helping Piper pour developing solutions into trays and then watched as the pictures magically appeared.

Piper had told Kate she was welcome to take any photo she wanted. Kate had picked two, a snapshot of Piper and the other of Marsh atop his horse, Apollo.

She'd kept the picture of Marsh in her wallet for a long time, unable to throw it away. After a few months, it had become dog-eared and faded, but she wondered what Marsh would think if he knew she'd carried it around for so long.

"I'll go check on Sabrina," she said, crossing to the door.

"Wait a minute!" he said. "Tell me. How did you know my sister's name was Piper?"

Chapter Five

Kate felt the color rush to her cheeks at his question. She swallowed convulsively, guiltily relieved he couldn't see her face.

"I...uh...didn't you mention her name a minute ago?" Kate said, racking her brain to remember if he had indeed spoken Piper's name.

"No, I didn't," Marsh replied evenly, his bruised features creasing in a frown.

"Then I guess I must have seen her name somewhere in her room," Kate countered with more confidence than she was feeling.

Marsh nodded slowly, his features relaxing. "You're probably right," he commented, though he didn't sound convinced.

"Are you sure you don't want me to bring you anything—a cool drink?" Kate asked, hoping to distract him.

"I'll be fine," Marsh said in a quietly dismissive tone.

Kate silently withdrew, scolding herself for her inadvertent slip. Marsh might be blind, but there was nothing wrong with his mind. While she wasn't sure what his reaction would be if he discovered her identity, he had enough to contend with at the moment.

Kate walked down the hall to the room Marsh's parents had made ready for their granddaughter. She recalled Piper telling her that it had been a playroom when she and her brothers were growing up.

The room had undergone quite a transformation. A canopied bed, adorned with pink pillows and frills and a dozen stuffed animals, occupied pride of place in the center of the room. Beneath the window stood a tall bookshelf painted white, its shelves packed with a wondrous assortment of children's books. Next to the bookshelf was a small easel and chalkboard and an old wooden school desk.

Sabrina was sitting at the desk drawing on a piece of colored construction paper.

"Hi, Sabrina! What are you doing?" Kate asked as she crossed the gray-carpeted floor.

"Drawing a picture of my new house," Sabrina said flashing a smile.

"That's nice." Kate glanced at the drawing. Sabrina had drawn several squarish scrawls with a chimney on top. Inside one of the squares were three stick-like figures, two large and one small.

"Let me see," Kate said seriously. "Is that your daddy?" She pointed to the tallest of the two figures.

Sabrina nodded vigorously, making her hair dance around her shoulders. "I'm in the middle," she said using the crayon to demonstrate. "And that's you," she added, pointing to the second figure. "Almost like a real family," Sabrina commented before turning back to the drawing.

"Almost," Kate said in a throaty voice, recalling again her adolescent dreams.

"Do you like my picture?" Sabrina asked, gazing up at Kate with those startling blue eyes so like her father's.

"I love your picture. It's beautiful," Kate praised, and if her voice was husky, she was the only one who noticed.

Sabrina slid the picture off the desktop and turned to her. "You can have it if you like," she

said her expression one of sweetness and inno-
cence.

Kate had to blink away the moisture suddenly
stinging her eyes. "Don't you want to give it to
your daddy?"

Sabrina regarded her with a puzzled frown.
"Daddy can't see, remember?"

Kate had to struggle not to smile at the child's
simple but unmistakable logic. "How could I forget," Kate said. "Thank you, Sabrina," she said
taking the drawing. "I'll treasure it always."

An hour later Kate rapped loudly on Marsh's
bedroom door.

"Yes!" His voice, though muffled, held more
than a trace of annoyance.

Kate entered with Sabrina by her side. "Dr. Diamond, it's Sabrina and me," she said brightly.

Marsh lay on the bed, his eyes closed. He'd removed his shoes and his jacket and unbuttoned his
shirt, revealing a small expanse of his tanned chest.

Ignoring the wild flutter of her pulse, Kate approached the bed. "How's your headache? Did
you manage to sleep?"

"About the same, and no I didn't sleep."

"Sabrina and I were wondering if you were hungry," Kate said, her gaze drawn to the smattering
of dark hair just visible in the vee of his shirt.

"We had milk and cookies," Sabrina told him cheerfully. "Want us to bring you some, Daddy?"

"I'm not hungry," Marsh's reply was brusque to the point of rudeness, and in response to his harsh tone, Sabrina's lip began to quiver. "What time is it?"

"Four o'clock," Kate answered. "What time would you like to eat dinner?"

"Whenever you like. You're in charge. I assume the supermarket delivered the food I ordered."

"Yes, they did. And someone unpacked it all and put it away."

"That was probably Hank Wilson, he's the stable manager. I talked to him earlier this morning."

"Is there anything special you'd like me to cook for you and Sabrina tonight?" Kate asked, thinking it would be nice to celebrate in some small way his and Sabrina's first meal at the ranch.

"I'm really not very hungry. I just want to be left in peace. Is that too much to ask?"

Annoyance rippled through Kate at his response. She glanced again at Sabrina in time to see tears pool in her pretty blue eyes.

"Sabrina, sweetheart, why don't you go to your room and play," Kate suggested, wanting to shield the child from her father's obvious ill humor.

Sabrina looked relieved, and with a quick glance

at her father on the bed, she bolted from the room like a horse out of the starting gate.

Kate turned to the man reclining on the bed. She was about to give him a piece of her mind, to tell him that he shouldn't take his frustration out on his daughter, that Sabrina deserved better, but when she saw the look of pain on his bruised face, the words died in her throat.

"Is your headache worse?" she asked, concern in her voice.

"Yes," came the abrupt response. He grimaced and began to massage his temple.

"Did Dr. Franklin give you some painkillers?"

"Yes, they're in my jacket pocket."

Kate picked up the navy sports jacket he'd tossed across the bed. She located the container of pills and shook two into her hand. "I'll get a glass of water from the bathroom."

By the time she returned, Marsh had eased himself into a sitting position.

"Open your mouth."

He complied, and she placed the pills on his tongue. "Here's the water." She brought the glass to his lips.

When his hand came up to cover hers, the warmth from his fingers sent her pulse into overdrive. She held her breath as she waited for him to swallow the medication.

Marsh sagged against the pillows. His head was throbbing like a pneumatic drill on a city sidewalk. He hadn't slept. He hadn't even dozed. He'd simply lain on top of the bed thinking how much he hated feeling so totally and utterly helpless.

The blackness was decidedly claustrophobic, making him feel as though he'd been buried alive. With each passing minute the urge to lash out and scream his frustration threatened to overwhelm him, and he had to fight to contain his anger and slow his thundering heartbeat.

"Take a deep breath. Try to relax," he heard Kate say in a tone that was soft and soothing. "Would you like more water?"

Marsh shook his head. He took her advice and inhaled deeply, and suddenly he was bombarded by the scent of jasmine.

"Dr. Diamond…"

"Please, my name's Marsh," he said with a tired sigh, beginning to feel the painkillers kick in.

"Marsh." She spoke his name tentatively, almost as if she was reluctant to say it. "I know this is difficult for you, but it is temporary. You will get your sight back. You have to remember that and be patient."

Her lilting voice acted like a balm, and silently Marsh acknowledged what she said was true. But he had a reputation for having a shotgun temper, which at times had gotten him in trouble. Patience was one virtue he'd never quite mastered.

"You're right, I know. But it's so damned difficult...."

He'd hoped that coming home to the ranch, to what would be more familiar surroundings, would alleviate some of the stress caused by his blindness.

But nothing had changed. He was still immersed in an alien world that left him uncharacteristically vulnerable, and more frightened than he was willing to admit.

Needing a distraction, he shifted his attention to the woman standing nearby. What did Kate look like? Was she blond or brunette? A redhead, perhaps? What color were her eyes? How old was she? How tall? Was she skinny or full figured?

From the clear and youthful tone of her voice, he guessed she was probably in her twenties. Probably late twenties, judging by her ease with Sabrina and her patient demeanor.

Suddenly he recalled the way she'd supported his weight in the hospital room, preventing him from falling. Strong, yet slender, with a body that was unmistakably feminine.

He felt his body tense in reaction, and suddenly another sensation, strangely familiar, engulfed him.

He frowned, struggling to unearth the elusive

memory, but his mind kept drifting as the pain-killers worked their magic.

"Marsh? Are you all right?" He heard concern in Kate's voice.

"I'm okay," he assured her after a momentary pause. "The pills are working. My headache is easing up. I didn't sleep before, but now I think I might take a nap."

"Good idea. I'll check on you in a little while."

Kate slowly withdrew, closing the door behind her. As she'd stood by his bedside watching him, she'd seen an array of troubling emotions flit across his face.

She'd longed to reach out and touch him, soothe away the lines of worry. She was pleased to note that the bruising around his eyes—though highly colorful—appeared to be less severe.

Kate headed down the hallway to Sabrina's room, where she found the little girl curled up on her bed fast asleep. Kate felt a pain squeeze her heart when she noticed Sabrina's wet lashes and the track of dried tears on her cheeks.

Retreating once more, Kate made her way to the kitchen. After unwrapping several packages, she opted to cook four plump chicken breasts, accompanied by broccoli and a green salad.

Gathering the items she would need, Kate set to work.

She'd barely begun when a knock startled her, and she turned to see a tall man wearing jeans and a white T-shirt enter through the back door. He removed his Stetson and nodded in greeting.

"Excuse me, ma'am," he drawled. "My name is Hank Wilson. I'm the stable manager."

"Hello, Mr. Wilson." Kate smiled at the newcomer, a man in his mid-fifties with thinning brown hair and a face tanned and leathered by the outdoors. "I'm Kate Turner. I'm the nurse Dr. Diamond hired to look after him and his daughter for a few days."

"Glad to meet you, ma'am. I hope you found everything all right. Dr. Diamond called this morning to say he'd ordered some supplies sent out. When they arrived, I had one of the men unload everything and put away the perishable items."

"He did a fine job."

"If you should need anything else, ma'am, just let me know. Me and the other stable hands live in the bunkhouse down by the stables. But you just have to dial 250 on the phone there—" he used his hat to point to the phone on the counter "—and you'll get me or one of my men."

"Thank you. I'll tell Dr. Diamond you came by." Kate knew the stables and living quarters were an entity unto themselves, but she had to smile at Hank using the word bunkhouse. The building was more like a small hotel.

"Uh…ma'am, speaking of Dr. Diamond, how is he? We were mighty sorry to hear about the accident. Is it true, I mean, is the doctor really blind?" the manager asked as he shifted from one foot to the other, obviously a little ill at ease.

"Yes, it's true. But his condition is only temporary. Once the swelling goes down he'll be back to normal."

"That's good news. The boss…that is Spencer, Dr. Diamond's brother, called late last night about Queenie, that's Queen of the North, one of his prize mares. She's due to drop her foal in a couple of weeks. I told him about the accident, not that I could tell him much, mind you, and he said he'd try to get through to the hospital, or failing that he'd call back again tonight."

"Thanks, I'll pass that news along to Dr. Diamond."

"Well, I'd best be getting back to work. Don't forget, if you need anything, you just have to call."

After Hank left, Kate finished preparing the salad. She coated the chicken breasts in seasoned breadcrumbs, placed them on a baking tray and put them in the oven.

Returning upstairs, she went first to Sabrina's room and found the child sitting on the floor near the bookshelf, leafing through one of numerous picture books.

"Sabrina, you're awake! Did you have a nice nap?"

Sabrina nodded and continued to flip the pages.

"What are you reading?" Kate asked lowering herself to the floor beside Sabrina. "Oh, it's a book of nursery rhymes. They're my favorites," she said. "Would you like me to read it to you?"

Sabrina threw Kate a startled glance. "You want to read it to me?"

"Of course," Kate replied, puzzled by Sabrina's reply. "I love reading books aloud, especially nursery rhymes."

"You do?" The child's expression was one of bewilderment. "Mommy never read me stories. She said they were silly. So I just look at the pictures."

Kate felt her heart contract. How could a mother refuse to read to her child? One of her most cherished memories was of sitting in her mother's lap listening to her soft lilting voice as she read to her. She wished she still owned some of those books, especially the one about a lost puppy searching for its mother. No matter how many times she'd asked her mother to read the story, she would always smile, stop whatever she was doing and gather Kate in her arms.

"I like looking at the pictures, too," Kate said easily, not wanting Sabrina to think she'd missed out on anything. "But now that you're older, reading the words makes it even better. Why don't you sit on my lap, and we'll give it a try."

Sabrina gazed up at Kate, a look of uncertainty in her blue eyes. "Mommy didn't like me sitting on her lap, she said I might get her dirty."

"Did your mommy wear pretty dresses all the time?" Kate asked, her heart aching for Sabrina, wondering why Marsh's wife had bothered to have a child.

"Uh-huh."

"Well, that explains it. You see I didn't bring any of my pretty dresses with me. These slacks and my blouse are part of my nurse's uniform. I'm allowed to get my uniform dirty, so it's all right to sit on my lap."

Sabrina didn't need a second invitation and listened, enthralled, as Kate read the nursery rhymes.

"Can you read them again?"

Kate glanced at her watch and saw that it was five-thirty. "How about we read it at bedtime? Right now I think we should check on your father again. Maybe he's hungry. I know I am," she added as she eased Sabrina from her lap and stood up.

"Do we have to?" Sabrina asked, obviously reluctant to brave the lion's den.

"I know your daddy is a bit grumpy. But he isn't mad at you, he's just mad because he can't see."

"Oh..." Sabrina said. "First, I have to go to the bathroom."

"Fine. Don't forget to wash your hands," she added as she headed toward Marsh's room.

As she drew near she heard a crash from inside. Without bothering to knock, she opened the door in time to see Marsh emerging rather drunkenly from the ensuite bathroom.

"Dr. Dia— Marsh? What happened? I heard a crash. Are you all right?" she asked, crossing to his side.

"I'm fine. I knocked something down in there."

Kate noticed as she led him to the bed, that his hands were wet. "The bed's beside you. I'll get a towel." She walked into the bathroom and surveyed the damage.

He'd obviously been trying to wash his hands and, in his search for the towel hanging on a rail nearby, he'd accidentally knocked an array of toiletries off a glass shelf onto the floor.

Kate quickly gathered the scattered items. Luckily nothing was broken.

"Here's the towel," she said, and placed it in his hands.

Marsh closed his fist around it, then before Kate could stop him he threw it on the floor. "Damn it all! Why is this happening to me? I should never have come here! I should have stayed in Chicago, and then none of this would be happening!"

"Marsh! You mustn't do this to yourself!" Distressed by the despair she could hear in his voice, Kate put her arm around his shoulders.

Heat chased up her arm and a tingling awareness darted through her, but she ignored it. Her heart ached for him, but while he had every right to be angry at his predicament, he needed to get a handle on his frustration, not only for his own sake but also for Sabrina's.

"Daddy? What's the matter?" Sabrina's anxious voice cut through the silence, and Kate glanced up to see her pale face and fearful expression.

"Your father knocked some things over in his bathroom, and hurt his arm," Kate answered for him, worried that Marsh, in his present state, might snap at Sabrina again.

"Did he break something? Mommy always got upset when she broke things."

Kate felt Marsh's shoulders rise and fall in a sigh. "Nothing's broken. Listen, Sabrina, dinner's almost ready, and I could use your help to set the table,'' Kate said, feeling it would be best to leave and let Marsh regroup.

"Are you coming downstairs for dinner, Daddy?"

Marsh drew a steadying breath. "I think I'll pass."

"You should eat something," Kate countered. "I'll bring up a tray."

"Fine."

"Come on, Sabrina. You can help me make up a tray for your father."

"I sure hope Daddy feels better soon," Sabrina said as she scampered down the hall.

Chapter Six

"**I**s my daddy really going to see again?" Sabrina asked as she carried the salt and pepper to the kitchen table where she'd already set out place-mats and cutlery for two.

"Of course," Kate replied as she cut one of the chicken breasts in two, then into bite-size pieces for Sabrina. Reaching for the salad bowl, she scooped a serving onto each of the three plates.

"Hop up at the table," Kate said with a smile, setting one of the plates in front of Sabrina. "Eat up. I'll take this tray up to your father."

"Can I have a drink of milk, please?"

"I'll pour us both a glass when I get back."

Kate quickly made her way upstairs. On reaching Marsh's room she balanced the tray on one hand, knocked and entered.

"I brought you dinner," she said, crossing to the bed. "It's chicken. I cut it into bite-size pieces for you."

"I'm really not hungry."

"You haven't eaten a thing since we got here. I think you're afraid—"

"Afraid of what?"

Kate smiled. No man liked to be told he was afraid of anything. "We all take it for granted that we can see what we're eating," she stated calmly, setting the tray on his lap. "My bet is you don't want to eat in front of Sabrina and me because you're afraid you'll miss your mouth or pour milk down your chin."

Marsh made no comment, but the expression on his face told her she was right on the mark.

"This way you can eat in private. Think of the plate as a clock face. The chicken is located between twelve and four, the broccoli between four and eight and the salad eight and twelve.

"The glass of milk might pose a slight problem. I only filled it half-full. You'll find it at the one o'clock position on the tray, to the right of your dinner plate. If you want to use the fork, you'll have to find it yourself," she added in a teasing voice. "Oh...and one last thing... here's a nap-

kin.'' She placed the cloth napkin in his right hand.
''Enjoy!''

Marsh listened to the sound of Kate's footsteps
receding. He silently berated himself for behaving
like such a grumpy bear to her and Sabrina. But
now he wasn't sure whether he should be annoyed
at her or simply give in to the urge to laugh.

Suddenly he was starving. His stomach growled
in confirmation. Kate had been right, about everything. He hadn't wanted to make a fool of himself,
having discovered at the hospital that morning that
feeding himself was something of a challenge.

The pieces of chicken were exactly where Kate
had said, and as he savored the taste he silently
gave thanks for her straightforward, uncompromis-
ing approach.

''I see you were hungry after all,'' Kate said
when she returned half an hour later to collect the
tray. The plate was completely empty, the milk
gone.

''I didn't want to waste either the food or your
efforts cooking it,'' Marsh replied easily. ''Thank
you. It was delicious,'' he added.

''You're welcome,'' Kate said, warmed by his
words. ''By the way, your suitcases are outside in
the hall. Do you want me to unpack them for
you?''

"If you'd put them in the closet for now, I'll unpack tomorrow."

Just as he finished speaking, the telephone rang.

"I bet that's your brother. I forgot to mention earlier that Hank Wilson came by and introduced himself. He said your brother called last night and, when he heard about your accident, said he might call back again tonight.

"There's no phone in here, is there? I'll run downstairs," Kate added and quickly hurried from the room.

Kate answered the phone on the fourth ring, noting as she did that it was a portable model. After introducing herself to Spencer, she carried the phone upstairs and put the receiver into Marsh's hand.

"Hello, Spencer! How's Ireland?" Marsh asked in a cheery voice.

"Green and wet. What's this I hear about you being in an accident? Are you and Sabrina all right? What gives, little brother?"

"Sabrina's fine. I got a few cuts and bruises, but I'm okay, at least for the most part."

"Then why the nurse?"

"I'm having a little trouble with my eyesight."

"How much trouble? Blurred vision, double vision, what?"

Marsh's hand tightened around the phone, and

his body tensed. He should have known Spencer wouldn't let him off the hook. "I'm blind."

"Blind? My God, Marsh, what's minor about that?" His brother sounded agitated.

"Because it's only temporary. I hit my head on the steering wheel, resulting in some swelling and bruising. Once that goes away, I should be as good as new. I hired a nurse because there was no one here to take care of Sabrina."

"I see. Listen, I'm sure Mom and Dad would fly home tomorrow if you want them to."

"By the time they get here things will be back to normal, and they'll have cut short their trip for nothing."

"If you're sure…"

"I'm sure. What time is it with you?" he asked, changing the subject.

"Almost two in the morning. Why?"

"That's a late night, even for you," Marsh teased. "Unless, of course, it was a woman who kept you out this late."

"The only females I'm interested in are of the four-legged variety, especially ones who run like the wind. Take care, little brother. I'll talk to you soon."

Marsh fumbled with the handset in search of the disconnect button. He sat for a moment thinking about his older brother, wondering if Spencer would ever get over his wife's death in a car accident two years ago.

Since then Spencer had pretty well steered clear of relationships, and Marsh thought it was time his older brother stopped grieving, found himself a woman and settled down to start a family of his own.

Ha! Marsh snorted silently. Who was he to suggest his brother find someone and get married? He hadn't done such a hot job of finding the right woman himself, or of making his marriage work.

On reflection he saw now that his mistake had been in believing Tiffany when she'd told him she wanted the same things he did from a relationship, from a marriage.

She'd captivated him with her beauty, her poise and her sophistication. If he'd delved deeper, he would have realized that she was shallow, spoiled and insincere. The fact that he'd been rising quickly through the hospital administration ranks had been a major factor. She'd simply seen him as a prize, a trophy to win. She'd reeled him in without a struggle.

He'd been a fool. A blind, stupid fool. He laughed aloud, the bitter, hollow sound reverberating in his ears.

As Kate emerged from the bathroom where

she'd been running a bath for Sabrina, she heard laughter coming from Marsh's room.

She stopped. The laughter was neither joyous nor happy, leaving Kate feeling sad and troubled. When she'd known him ten years ago, he'd been friendly and fun, patient and kind, helping her get over her fear of horses.

She'd admired him tremendously for the way he always looked out for his sister, and for his driving ambition to become a doctor.

The Marshall Diamond she'd known back then would have regarded his temporary blindness not only as a challenge but also as a learning experience. By giving in to his anger and frustration he was pushing away the person who needed him most, his daughter.

Sabrina was a beautiful little girl, eager to be loved and accepted. Like any child her age, she responded to praise, encouragement and love.

But Kate had a hunch Sabrina hadn't been afforded these essential elements thus far in her life, and Kate knew there was a real danger that if Marsh turned away from his daughter now, Sabrina would be lost to him forever.

By the middle of the week she could see daily that the gap between father and daughter was widening. She feared the damage he'd already inflicted might well be irreversible.

He never left his bedroom, and any attempt Kate or Sabrina made to entice him into coming downstairs failed. Marsh wasn't interested in making adjustments, learning how to cope with his condition. He was simply waiting, none too patiently, for his sight to return.

Kate was finding it increasingly difficult to curb her tongue. Marsh was behaving like a spoiled child, sulking in his room waiting for his punishment to be over.

As a nurse, she'd had to deal with a variety of people with numerous illnesses. She'd constantly been amazed, humbled and deeply moved by the way most people coped with their situations, some with quiet perseverance, others challenging without complaint almost insurmountable odds.

In Marsh's case the odds were in his favor. His sight would return. Instead of making the best of a bad situation, he'd chosen to make everyone's life miserable.

Whenever Kate and Sabrina ventured into the "lion's den," as Kate had come to regard Marsh's bedroom, Sabrina usually did so with great reluctance.

During those first few days, Kate had encouraged Sabrina to take things up to her father, hoping he'd ask his daughter to keep him company or offer to tell her a story. But Sabrina usually returned to the kitchen within minutes, her unhappy expression telling Kate all she needed to know.

The first time Sabrina reappeared, Kate had seen a glint of tears in the child's eyes. She'd been halfway up the stairs to take Marsh to task before sanity prevailed.

To compensate for her father's neglect, Kate had made it a point to involve Sabrina in everything. As a result, the child rarely left Kate's side. Now a deep bond had formed between them.

From the comments Sabrina made and the questions she asked, Kate realized that the child's apprehensive wariness in her father's presence had everything to do with what her mother had told her. Obviously, Marsh's wife had wanted to destroy Sabrina's relationship with her father and his family.

But while Kate sympathized with his predicament, she was fast losing patience with him.

"Sabrina, if you carry the bowl of ice cream up to your father's room, I won't have to make a second trip," Kate said as she put the finishing touches to Marsh's dinner tray a few nights later.

"Do I have to?"

Kate bit back a sigh. "No, you don't have to. If you help, though, I'll be finished sooner, and then we can go outside and play ball like you wanted."

Sabrina's eyes brightened with interest and anticipation. "Okay," she said sliding off her chair at the kitchen table.

Kate handed Sabrina the bowl of ice cream and the spoon. "Thanks, you're a great helper," she praised as she led the way from the kitchen.

"We've brought dinner," Kate announced as they entered Marsh's bedroom. "I have the main course here on the tray, and Sabrina, who has been such a big help to me today, has brought dessert," she added brightly, hoping Marsh might at the very least thank his daughter for her contribution.

"It's chocolate chip ice cream," Sabrina told her father as she approached the easy chair where Marsh spent most of his time.

"You can take the ice cream back, I don't like it," Marsh said in the gruff voice Kate had come to hate.

"Nonsense. Everyone likes ice cream," Kate countered, annoyance rippling through her when she saw Sabrina's eyes fill with tears.

"Not me!" Marsh said, and at his sharp reply Kate watched helplessly as Sabrina threw the bowl on the floor, before turning and running from the room.

"What was that? Did you drop something?" Marsh asked, oblivious to the fact that his comment had upset his daughter. "I hope it wasn't my dinner. What's on the menu tonight?"

Kate stood staring after Sabrina. Damn the man! How could he be such an insensitive boor! Sabrina had only been trying to help, and he'd tossed his daughter's efforts back in her face just like he'd done to Kate the night at the lake when she'd helped Piper.

She'd wanted to rage at him then for jumping to conclusions, for refusing to listen to her explanation, but foolishly she'd kept silent... Not this time...

"Bread and water!" Kate replied abruptly as the anger she'd been struggling to hold on to broke free. "After that little display, it's all you deserve."

Marsh seemed taken aback by her outburst. "I don't understand."

"Then maybe it's time I explained." Kate set the tray down on the chest of drawers nearby. "Your daughter just ran out of here in tears," she told him as she crouched to pick up the bowl and ice cream from the carpet.

"Tears? Why?" He sounded genuinely surprised.

"Why?" Kate repeated, her tone incredulous. She stood up, and for a moment was tempted to drop the ice cream on his head. "Ever since we set foot in this house you've been sulking in your room waiting for your sight to return. In the meantime, your daughter, who has been through quite a bit herself lately in case you've forgotten, has already begun to distance herself from you. I think she's afraid of you.

"What if your blindness is permanent?" Kate hurried on before Marsh could reply. "What if you have to spend the rest of your life this way? Would you just sit here in your room waiting to die? Or would you snap out of it, take control of your life and learn to live with your disability?

"You're lucky! Because you're going to get your eyesight back," she raged at him. "But in the meantime, while you're busy feeling sorry for yourself, you're doing irreparable damage to your relationship with your daughter.

"Sabrina needs you, Marsh. She needs your love and attention. She lost her mother a few months ago, and she almost lost you in that accident. She's feeling lost and lonely and very vulnerable, and if you continue to turn away from her, the way you've been doing...if you keep ignoring her and criticizing her every time she approaches you, you're going to lose her completely.

"I think it's time you stopped thinking about yourself and started thinking about her!"

Chapter Seven

Breathless, her heart pounding, Kate waited for Marsh to say something, anything. She knew she'd stepped out of line. Knew she had no right to berate him for the way he'd been behaving. But she could no more have kept quiet than she could fly to the moon.

He hadn't seen the look of pain and rejection in Sabrina's eyes when he'd told her he didn't like ice cream. He might just as well have told his daughter he didn't like her, because that's how the child had reacted.

The air crackled with tension as the silence stretched between them like a yawning void.

"Are you quite finished?" Marsh asked, his anger quietly contained.

"For now," Kate replied with a hint of defiance, unsure just how to gauge his response.

"Do you always give your patients a lecture?"

"Only the ones who need it. Do you still want dinner?" she asked, thinking it best to shift gears.

She retrieved the tray and set it on his lap, but before she could withdraw, his hand captured hers. She drew a startled breath as a frisson of heat sprinted up her arm, and a different tension, both intoxicating and exciting, sizzled between them.

He leaned toward her, bringing his face within inches of hers. Kate could feel his breath on her cheek, smell the evocative male scent that was his alone, a scent that stirred her senses unbearably, leaving her with an ache she knew only he could appease.

"I'll say this," he drawled in that deep resonant tone that made her go weak at the knees. "You've given me food for thought." As he spoke, his thumb absently caressed the underside of her wrist causing even more havoc.

"Good," Kate managed to respond, her voice heavy with emotion. Tiny ripples of sensation spiraled through her, awakening needs she hadn't felt in too long. His nearness and his touch were affecting her profoundly, creating a heat that was spreading to every cell.

During the past few days she'd subjected herself

to several close encounters with Marsh. In her capacity as a nurse she'd had to check his stitches, change his dressing as well as rebandage his sprained wrist, and on each occasion she'd been made agonizingly aware of his potent masculinity and her body's intense reaction to him.

Hard as she'd tried to maintain a detached and professional relationship, she'd found herself having to fight the almost irresistible urge to rake her hands through his thick dark hair, kiss the taut line of his jaw or explore the tanned, contoured width of his shoulders.

It was ironic indeed, but she'd been glad he couldn't see her or her response. Yet was he aware of the tension vibrating through her now?

"I'd better check on Sabrina," Kate said, intent on breaking free of his hold.

"By all means." Kate almost sagged with relief when he released her. "It is what I'm paying you for."

"You're right. It is."

"Take the tray with you. I'm not hungry."

Without further ado, Kate scooped up the tray and quickly made her escape.

Marsh sat for several long seconds waiting for his anger to recede. He was still reeling from her scathing discourse, but he was man enough to acknowledge that she was right. There really was no excuse for his blatantly selfish behavior these last few days, or for hiding in his bedroom and deliberately ignoring his own daughter.

Yes, he'd had a few curve balls thrown his way in the past year, this recent one being the most devastating. But he was an adult, for heaven's sake! A man of thirty-seven, and as such, better equipped emotionally to deal with life's traumas than an innocent, defenseless, five-year-old.

He'd been wallowing in self-pity, waiting, none too patiently, for his eyesight to return and taking his growing frustration out on Sabrina and Kate. He hadn't been a model patient by any stretch of the imagination. Yet Kate had quietly gone about her business without complaint. Until now. She'd only taken him to task because of the way he'd treated Sabrina. And she'd been right to rage at him.

The accident had knocked his life off course, making him forget his main objective in coming to Kincade, which was to break down the barriers his daughter had erected. But instead of following through on the vow he'd made to work toward a closer relationship with Sabrina, he'd been pushing her farther and farther away. And if he didn't stop obsessing about getting his sight back, he could remain forever locked in this prison of his own making.

* * *

"Kate? Sabrina?" Marsh called out as he emerged from the bathroom dressed in his terry cloth bathrobe. He thought he'd heard voices in the hallway.

He'd spent the past hour, since Kate left him, exploring his bedroom, stepping out the distances between the door and the bed, in every possible direction. He now knew the location of each item of furniture in the room. He'd banged his shins several times, and he'd knocked a few items off the dresser. But he'd persisted. Already he felt more confident and in control. And after taking a shower, he'd been both pleased and proud at his efforts. For the first time since arriving at the ranch, he was starting to feel like his old self.

Kate rapped lightly on Marsh's door. She was feeling a little guilty at her rather rude outburst and she wanted to check that he was all right.

"Kate? Is that you?" Marsh asked as he opened the bedroom door.

"Yes," she replied, surprised to find him standing there. For a fleeting second she had the distinct impression he could see her. He was looking right at her, and she felt her heart tighten against her breastbone in startled reaction.

He was wearing a bathrobe, and his hair looked damp and disheveled.

"What time is it?" His question filled the awkward silence.

"Seven-thirty."

"Is Sabrina asleep?"

"Yes, I just—"

"Good. Come in. We need to talk." His tone was serious, and Kate's heart plummeted. Was he going to fire her?

Marsh stepped back, then turned, and Kate watched in fascination as he walked with confidence toward the easy chair.

Kate followed, and inhaled the lemony scent of soap and shampoo. Suddenly, the realization that Marsh had recently showered, and that beneath his burgundy robe he was quite probably naked, registered.

She swallowed convulsively as a tingling awareness rippled through her. What would it feel like to have his naked body pressed urgently against hers? she wondered.

Heat suffused her face as an erotic image of the two of them, their bodies entangled in a sensual embrace, flashed into her mind.

Drawing a deep, steadying breath, Kate reined in her lustful thoughts, silently berating herself. Surely, after all these years she wasn't still carrying a torch for Marsh? Especially after the callous way he'd treated her and now Sabrina?

"I've made a decision," Marsh said, coming quickly to the point.

"I see," Kate responded, struggling to keep her tone light, not wanting to give even a hint of the disappointment washing over her.

"I've been thinking about what you said. And you're absolutely right. It *is* time I stopped wallowing in self-pity and started thinking about what my daughter needs." Kate could hear guilt and regret in his voice. "I came home to Kincade so that Sabrina and I could make a fresh start. I just hope it's not too late...." His voice trailed off.

Kate felt her heart contract at his words.

"It's never too late. I know Sabrina is concerned and a little frightened by all that's happened, but children have a tremendous capacity to bounce back. All they need is to know they're loved and wanted."

Marsh's features creased into a small frown. "Sounds to me as though you're talking from personal experience, Kate. Are you?"

Kate felt her heart skip a beat. "What makes you ask?"

"Something in your voice. Did you have a rough childhood?"

Kate heard the compassion in his voice, and for

a moment she was tempted to say "yes." But the shame of being raised by an alcoholic father who'd ignored and neglected her remained with her like a festering wound. "My childhood's not the issue," Kate quickly asserted, silently hoping he wouldn't pursue the matter.

"I'm sorry. I didn't mean to pry. You're absolutely right." Marsh paused. "It's becoming rather an annoying habit...you being right, I mean." His voice was laced with humor.

"You just proved the old adage about doctors making the worst patients. Besides, it hasn't exactly been easy for you, waking up to discover you can't see."

"No, it hasn't been easy." Marsh sighed and ran his right hand through his wet hair, an action that loosened the belt on his robe. Casually he gathered the ends of the fabric together, but not before Kate caught a glimpse of a smattering of dark hairs on his chest.

A hot wave of awareness washed across her skin, leaving a trail of need behind.

"Where's your sling?" she asked, attempting to distract herself. "Is your arm feeling better?"

"Yes, it is. Thankfully, it wasn't a bad sprain." He paused, then walked to the dresser. Locating the handle for the top drawer, he pulled it open.

"I'd better get dressed. Would there by any chance be any dinner left?"

"Of course," Kate quickly assured him. She'd put his uneaten portion back in the fridge. "I could bring you a tray—"

"Actually, I thought I might venture downstairs for a while," he said. "With your help, of course."

"I'd be happy to," Kate replied, unable to keep the smile from her voice.

"Why don't you come back in about ten minutes?" he suggested.

"That was delicious, thank you," Marsh said as he finished off the piece of apple pie Kate had served him. It felt good to be out of his room. He hadn't realized just how cooped up he'd been feeling.

He'd managed the trip downstairs with relative ease, but Kate deserved credit for making the journey a smooth one. She'd talked him through it, her matter-of-fact, no-nonsense tone giving him the confidence he needed.

"Would you like to sit outside for a while? It's such a beautiful evening."

"You must be a mind reader," Marsh said, thinking a dose of fresh air would do him a world of good.

Kate led him out to the veranda. "Have you

worked with blind people before?'' Marsh asked once he was safely seated in the old wooden garden swing that his father had built when they were children.

''Yes,'' Kate replied. ''My ex-husband and I lived next door to an elderly lady who was going blind. Mrs. Kemp was determined to manage on her own, to be totally independent, and so she took a course put on especially for the newly blind,'' she went on. ''I thought it would help me with my nurse's training, so I asked if I could observe.''

As Marsh gently rocked the garden swing, he noted with silent admiration how Kate had managed to watch over her neighbor without the woman ever feeling that she'd lost any of her independence.

During the short time she'd been in his employ, he'd ascertained Kate was a generous, unselfish and hardworking young woman who had a knack with both children and adults.

Her mention of an ex-husband only added to the intrigue surrounding her. He was surprised her marriage had failed and was tempted, for a moment to ask what went wrong. But he refrained, knowing firsthand how easily a relationship could go sour, how quickly love and trust could be wiped out.

Marsh inhaled deeply, drawing in an array of scents from the flowers his mother planted each spring in the hanging baskets around the veranda, to the familiar and much-loved smell of horseflesh and freshly mowed grass.

"Do you ride?" Marsh suddenly asked, and heard her sharp intake of breath at the question.

"Yes, I ride," Kate replied, after a brief hesitation. He'd caught her completely off guard with his question. She'd been gazing down the grassy hillside past the security fence to the row of stables and paddocks in the valley below.

"I thought the fact that we were coming to California," he said, "to a place where she could ride and have her own horse would excite Sabrina. Now I doubt I'll get her near the stables, never mind a horse."

"Time and maybe the right inducement is all you need," Kate said. "If I remember correctly, I think Hank said something about one of your brother's horses foaling soon. Baby animals are always a strong draw for children."

"Kate, you're a genius!" Marsh said, his mouth curving into a smile that banished the shadows from his face. "As a matter of fact, I used that exact same approach years ago on a friend of my sister's."

Kate's breath caught in her throat, and her heart stumbled against her rib cage. Those had been the tactics he'd used ten years ago when he'd helped her overcome her fear of horses.

She'd only been three when her father had taken a job at a rodeo, cleaning out the stalls. Her mother had gotten a job at the food court and, unable to afford a baby-sitter, they'd decided Kate would be safe with her father.

Kate had had fun playing in the straw and helping her father. Growing tired, she'd crawled onto a pile of straw in one of the empty horse stalls and fallen asleep. She'd awakened an hour later expecting to find her father there, but instead, standing near her bed of straw was an enormous black horse, a frightening sight for a child. Kate had screamed for her father, a reaction that startled and unnerved the horse. The animal had snorted and stamped and neighed in noisy agitation, compounding Kate's growing hysteria. Her father had come to her rescue, calming both the big stallion and Kate, but from that moment on she'd been nervous around horses.

Until she came to Kincade. Much to Kate's embarrassment Piper had told Marsh about her fear. She'd expected him to laugh or make fun, but he'd done neither. Instead he'd invited her to the stable to see the new foal.

The idea of spending time alone with Marsh had overridden her reluctance to enter the stables. He'd been sweet and funny, relating stories of some of his own boyhood horse-related escapades.

Listening to his easy chatter, Kate had forgotten to be nervous. Marsh came to a halt at a stall with a mare and her foal and speaking softly, he'd entered the stall. At first the foal hid behind his mother, but soon he grew curious about the newcomer. Kate had to laugh as the foal nudged Marsh in an attempt to gain his attention.

Marsh grinned at her and held out his hand inviting Kate to join him. Mesmerized by his smile, she ignored the jittery feeling in her stomach and entered the stall.

Smiling encouragement, he'd taken her hand, clasping it firmly. The jitters had instantly evaporated. When the foal's soft nose pressed against her other hand, the fear she'd anticipated and expected hadn't materialized, instead she'd felt only delight and a sense of wonder.

Less than a week later she was riding with Marsh and Piper out to the lake.

"Kate? Kate you are still there? I know you didn't leave...." Marsh's anxious voice cut through her reverie.

"Yes. Yes, I'm here." She abandoned the railing where she'd been standing and quickly crossed to sit on the swing beside him. "Sorry, I was admiring the view. I'd forgotten how—" She broke off abruptly, silently chastising herself for her slip. She glanced at Marsh to see if he'd noticed.

"It's quite a sight isn't it?" Kate heard the whisper of longing in his voice. "I'm looking forward to seeing it myself, very soon."

Kate leaned closer. "You will," she assured him softly. Covering his hand with hers, she squeezed it gently in a gesture purely meant to comfort.

"Thanks, Kate, for everything," Marsh said covering her hand with his other one.

Kate's heart beat against her breast like a trapped animal trying to escape. "Even for the lecture?" she asked, unable to resist teasing him.

Marsh chuckled. "Especially for the lecture. Sabrina and I are lucky you were available to help us out." He smiled. "You know, if you didn't already have a nursing job in the new hospital wing, I'd be tempted to offer you a job here as a nanny."

Kate made no reply, silently wondering whether he'd still be willing to offer her the job if she revealed her identity. Somehow she doubted it.

Chapter Eight

The next morning, using the cane Dr. Franklin had given him at the hospital and dressed in cream-colored slacks and a navy golf shirt, Marsh made the journey downstairs to the kitchen for breakfast.

Kate supervised the descent, and as she glanced across the table at him, she thought he'd never looked better. She admired his new determination to face his problem head-on.

"How do you like your room, Sabrina?" Marsh asked.

"Fine," his daughter replied before biting into a piece of toast.

"Did you unpack your suitcase?"

"Yes," Sabrina answered, reaching for her glass of orange juice.

Marsh sighed and lapsed into silence.

"May I be excused?" Sabrina asked politely a few minutes later.

"Of course," Kate responded. "Don't forget we're going into town later. Your father has an appointment with Dr. Franklin."

"Okay," Sabrina replied before slipping from the chair and heading for the door.

"Well, that attempt at conversation went over like a lead balloon," Marsh grumbled once he was sure Sabrina was out of earshot.

Kate gathered the breakfast dishes and carried them to the dishwasher. "You just have to be patient."

Marsh sighed again. "Unfortunately patience is not one of my strong suits. What would you suggest I do? I'd appreciate your help."

Kate closed the dishwasher and returned to the table. She was warmed by his request, pleased he intended to bridge the gap. "Sabrina likes to help. You could ask her to fetch your shoes or find your hairbrush, any number of little things. You could even send her to the kitchen on an errand."

"Those are great ideas. Still, I get the impression she'll run off again as soon as she's done. How can I spend more time with her? I can't play board games or draw or do anything that requires me to see," Marsh replied, exasperation edging his tone.

"You could tell her a story. You must remember some of the stories your mother read to you when you were a child. Sabrina loves to sit and listen to stories. She'll sit for hours. Her favorite story right now is Cinderella. I think I've read it to her a dozen times."

Kate watched a smile flit across Marsh's bruised features. "Cinderella, you say. Hmm...I was more partial to adventurous tales, like *Treasure Island, Robin Hood* or *Aladdin.*"

"Any or all of those would be great," Kate commented, ignoring the effect his smile had on her.

"A story it is, then. What time is my appointment with Tom?"

"Eleven." Dr. Franklin had called early that morning inquiring about Marsh. When he'd learned there was no change in her patient's condition, the doctor had suggested coming in for a follow-up examination.

"I'd like to go upstairs. I think it's time I paid a visit to Sabrina's room."

"Good idea."

"Leave me outside her door, will you?" Marsh said, once they'd reached the upper landing. Kate slowed to a halt, took Marsh's hand and placed it on the doorframe. She tapped lightly on Sabrina's door and quickly withdrew.

"Daddy? What are you doing here?"

"I came to visit. May I come in?"

"Okay. I guess."

"I'm going to need your help. I don't want to trip or fall."

"What do I do?"

"Make sure there's nothing on the floor I can trip over. Then take my hand and lead me to your bed. Then I can tell you a story."

"Hi, Kate, Sabrina. It's nice to see you both again." Dr. Franklin said when he emerged from his office with Marsh at his side. "How are you liking your new home, Sabrina?"

"Fine," Sabrina replied shyly, dropping her chin onto her chest.

Kate glanced at Marsh and noted the anxiety tugging at the corner of his mouth. The purple bruises around his eyes were starting to fade, and other than the fact that his sight hadn't returned, the only indication he'd suffered an injury was the angry red scar on his forehead.

"I'm afraid I haven't been able to give Sabrina a tour of the ranch yet," Marsh said.

"There'll be lots of time for that once your eyesight returns," Tom said, giving Marsh a friendly pat on the back. "Keep me posted. I'll give you a call next week if I haven't heard from you before then to say your sight is back."

"Thanks, Tom."

Kate moved to Marsh's side and began to lead him toward the elevator.

"Are we going home now?" Sabrina asked as they rode down to the main floor.

"We don't have to go home," Marsh replied. "Would you like to go for a drive?"

"Where could we go?" Sabrina wanted to know.

"Well, we could ask Kate to drive through downtown, and then we'll take another route I know back to the ranch."

"Okay."

"You don't mind, do you, Kate?"

"No, I don't mind."

"What time is it?" Marsh asked.

"Almost noon," Kate replied as the elevator came to a halt.

"I'm hungry," Sabrina announced. "Can we stop for lunch?"

Kate felt Marsh's hold on her arm tighten, and she knew by his reaction the idea of stopping to eat somewhere had little appeal.

"We could pick up hamburgers at a drive-through and go on a picnic," Kate said brightly as she led him off the elevator.

"Yeah. A picnic! Can we, Daddy?"

Kate held her breath. From his tense demeanor, she guessed he wasn't thrilled by her suggestion.

"That sounds like a great idea," Marsh replied, surprising Kate and Sabrina. "And I know the perfect place for a picnic."

"Where?" Sabrina asked as they walked out through the automatic doors.

"Let's get the burgers first," Marsh said as Kate led the way to the car. "Is Betsy's Burgers still around?"

"Yes," she replied, getting Sabrina and Marsh settled into the car. "Are we all buckled up?" She turned to check on Sabrina and noticed Marsh was fumbling trying to find the strap of his seat belt.

"Here, I'll get it." Sliding toward him, she twisted in her seat and leaned across him to grab the seat belt. It refused to budge, and in that moment Kate was suddenly aware that she was practically sitting in Marsh's lap.

Her lungs froze, and she felt her stomach flutter in alarm as awareness spiraled through her. Panicked, she tugged frantically at the belt. It came free with a snap, and she scrambled back to lock it in place.

With trembling fingers she locked her own belt

into place and put the car into reverse. "Betsy's Burgers it is," she said, hoping Marsh wouldn't notice the waver in her voice.

Half an hour later Kate pulled out of Betsy's drive-through lane and back into the lunchtime traffic. Beside her on the wide seat was a brown paper bag containing hamburgers, fries, onion rings and several ice-cold drinks.

The smell of food was beginning to make her mouth water.

"Where to?" Kate glanced at the man in the passenger seat.

"There's a small lake on the property that's ideal. We spent a lot of time picnicking and swimming there when I was growing up. Take a right on Sixth Street, it's a couple of blocks down. Then head back to the ranch. As soon as you make the turn and drive under the Blue Diamond Ranch sign, there's a dirt road on your left. You can't miss it."

"Oh…you must mean Little Diamond Lake," Kate said her heart taking a giant leap.

"That's right. How do you know?"

"Ah…well…." Kate ground to a halt, then inspiration saved her. "There's a relief map of the ranch hanging in the hallway. I happened to be studying it just this morning, and I noticed the lake."

"Did you go swimming in it, Daddy?"

"Yes. All the time. At least until the summer—" He broke off abruptly, and Kate felt her heart ram against her ribs in reaction.

"Until what? Daddy?"

Kate was silent. She knew what Marsh had been thinking, knew he'd been about to say, *until Piper nearly drowned.*

"Oh…until I left to go to Chicago," she heard him say. "I haven't been to the lake in a long time."

"Are we there yet?" Sabrina asked a few minutes later as Kate pulled in beneath the diamond-shaped, wrought-iron sign depicting a galloping horse and rider.

"Almost," Kate responded as she made the turn down the dirt road leading to the lake.

She'd never been back since that fateful night. But during the past ten years she'd often thought about all that had happened, and especially of Marsh's cruel and unwarranted verbal attack on her.

Until that night she'd been under the impression Marsh had liked her, might even have been a little attracted to her. But he'd swiftly made it very clear she'd been wrong, about everything.

She and Piper had been in town to catch a

movie, and they'd accepted a ride back to the ranch from Alex Edwards and his friend, Jason Hardy, two seniors from school.

When Piper suggested they stop off at the lake, the guys had readily agreed. When Alex brought out the six-pack of beer from the trunk of his car, Kate had hastily declined to take one. Piper, however, had had no such inhibitions and soon she was asking for a second.

Piper was laughing and flirting with the guys while Kate looked on. She'd tried to caution her friend about the effects of alcohol on someone unaccustomed to drinking, but Piper was enjoying the attention and having too much fun.

The seniors kept pace with Piper, each drinking two beers. A tipsy Piper had giggled and pointed out there was no beer left.

Eager to continue the party, Alex and his friend had hopped into the car promising to return with more beer.

Glad to see them leave, Kate offered to walk with Piper back to the ranch house. But Piper hadn't wanted to go home. She'd suddenly announced she was going swimming. Kicking off her shoes, she'd pushed a protesting Kate aside and headed for the water.

Kate had stood on the shore watching Piper splash around. When Piper began to swim toward the deeper part of the lake, Kate called out to her friend to come back, but Piper ignored her.

Piper soon appeared to be having difficulty. When she'd slipped beneath the surface, Kate had instantly raced in after her. She'd just finished hauling Piper onto the shore when Marsh arrived.

When he noticed the empty beer bottles on the ground, he'd turned on Kate. And while she'd understood his anger at finding his sister in such a terrible state, he'd jumped to the erroneous conclusion that Kate had supplied the alcohol, and therefore Kate was the one to blame.

Without bothering to listen to her attempts to explain, he'd proceeded to tear into her, telling her she was just like her drunken bum of a father. That Piper didn't need friends like her. And he'd ordered her to stay away from his sister in the future.

"Wow! It's pretty here," Sabrina said, bringing Kate's wayward thoughts to a halt. "Are we going to stop here?"

"I was just looking for a shaded spot," Kate replied as she brought the car to a stop beneath a spreading old birch tree.

"If you check in the trunk you might find something we could sit on," Marsh suggested as he fumbled for the door handle. "But hurry up. The

smell of those burgers is driving me crazy,'' he
added with a rumble of humor.

She quickly pressed a button to close the car's
power windows before shutting off the motor.
Climbing out, the heat struck her like a blow. She
glanced around taking in the familiar sight. Nothing appeared to have changed.

"Sabrina, look around for a nice grassy area,
under a tree.''

"There's a pretty spot over there,'' Sabrina replied, pointing toward the edge of the water.

"Can you lead me there? I don't want to trip or
walk into the water.''

"Okay!'' Taking her father's hand, she headed
toward a clump of trees and bushes.

Kate smiled as she unlocked the trunk. Marsh
had been right. Inside she found a folded blanket.
Retrieving it, she closed the lid and, anxious to be
out of the direct sun, she hurried toward Marsh and
Sabrina where she spread the blanket on the dry
grass.

"You can sit down now, Daddy.''

"Mmm...this is delicious,'' Marsh mumbled a
few minutes later through a mouthful of hamburger. "I just hope the sauce isn't dripping off
my chin onto my shirt,'' he added with a rueful
grin.

Sabrina giggled. "There is a drop of sauce on

your chin, Daddy. Want me to wipe it off for you?"

"Yes, please." Hearing the delightful sound of his daughter's childish giggle had lightened Marsh's mood considerably.

Sabrina set her own burger down and picked up a napkin from the small pile nearby, then leaned toward her father.

"There, that's better," Sabrina said after gently wiping his chin.

"Thank you. You're a big helper."

"Really?" Sabrina replied, her tone cautious, telling him she wasn't sure she believed him.

"Really," he answered softly and sincerely, wishing he could see Sabrina's face, wishing he could reach out and haul her into his arms and hug her tight.

Kate watched the exchange between father and daughter and felt a pain squeeze her heart. Though he couldn't see his daughter's face, there was pleasure and pride in her expression. Marsh had just taken the first step toward a new beginning with Sabrina.

"Having a picnic was a wonderful idea, Kate. Thank you."

"I've always loved picnics," Kate said, wondering what he'd think if he knew how they reminded her of that special summer.

Shifting onto her knees, she began to gather the stray napkins and empty hamburger wrappers.

"Can we go for a walk along the water? Can I paddle?"

"I don't see why not," Marsh replied. "But you must promise to stay close to the water's edge."

"I promise," Sabrina said, already dropping down to take off her running shoes and socks.

"Kate, how far are we from the water?"

"Not far. I'll watch her, or we can paddle with her."

"Want to paddle with me, Daddy?"

"I'd love to…but—"

"Aw…please. I'll hold your hand, so you won't trip."

Marsh laughed. "It's a deal. But only if Kate comes, too," he added as he began to untie his laces.

"Fine by me."

Sabrina held tight to her father's hand as they walked toward the water's edge. Marsh had had the foresight to roll up his slacks. Kate had done the same.

"Wheeee…" Sabrina's squeal of pleasure as her feet touched the water brought a bubble of laughter to Kate's throat. Hand in hand they waded into the silky, cool waters.

An observer would readily assume they were a

family out for an afternoon of fun, and Kate knew in her heart that she could never forget these precious moments.

It would be too easy to believe they were a family...that she belonged. Ever since her mother's death, Kate had longed to be part of a loving family, of belonging. Ten years ago that had been the dream she'd secretly harbored; the dream that Marsh would look at her and see his future, that he would fall as hopelessly in love with her as she had with him.

Her fantasy hadn't stopped there. She'd dreamed they'd get married, have two beautiful children and live happily ever after.

Sabrina soon released her father's hand to start running and splashing on her own. Marsh continued to hold on to Kate's hand, and his expression showed that he wasn't totally at ease.

"Let's sit down and dry off, shall we?" Marsh suggested five minutes later.

Kate could see that Sabrina was about to protest, and she quickly intervened. "Sabrina, if you help me take your father back to the blanket, I can watch you from there."

Sabrina ran to her father's side and slid her hand into his. Together they covered the short distance back to the blanket.

Kate followed more slowly. This was the spot

where she'd hauled Piper out of the water. This was where Marsh had berated her all those years ago. She'd been young and insecure, afraid to stand up for herself, but not any longer. Why else would she have agreed to take on the job of looking after him?

"Remember to stay near the water's edge," Marsh cautioned before he sat down.

"Yes, Daddy," she replied before scampering off.

"Can you see her?" Marsh asked scarcely a minute later.

"Yes. It's shallow here, and the water doesn't start to get deep until you're in quite a ways."

Marsh frowned and was about to say something when Sabrina called to them.

"She's waving at you," Kate said, and Marsh lifted his hand to wave back.

Shifting into a more comfortable position, Marsh accidentally brushed against Kate, and her heart skipped a beat at the contact.

"This was always one of my favorite places when I was growing up," Marsh said on a sigh. "It's funny but I don't really mind not being able to see it. I can see it clearly in my head."

"You're lucky to have had a spot like this," Kate commented, glancing to where Sabrina was crouched at the water's edge studying something at her feet.

"I know. Unfortunately there are some bad memories associated with the lake." At his words, Kate held her breath and shifted her gaze to look at him. "My sister nearly drowned out there."

Kate swallowed convulsively, surprised Marsh had brought up the incident. Had he guessed her identity?

"That must have been frightening," Kate said, though her voice sounded strange and distant.

"It has to be all of ten years ago, now." Marsh continued, his expression thoughtful. "But, I tell you, it's not something you ever forget."

"I guess not."

"Piper made a mistake that night. And as it turned out so did I," he added in a voice tinged with regret.

"You made a mistake? I don't understand," Kate said, intrigued by his comment and unable to let it go.

"Piper wasn't alone that night. She had a friend with her. Her name was Kat."

Kate froze. Kat was the nickname Piper had given her when they'd first met. Piper had teased her saying she reminded her of a little wild cat, always hissing and spitting.

Afraid to move or speak, she remained silent, praying he'd continue.

"I was on my way home when I decided to drive by the lake. Kat flagged me down, and when I saw Piper soaking wet and lifeless on the ground, I thought I was too late. I immediately went to work on her, giving her mouth-to-mouth, and she started coughing and gagging. She was alive! That was all that mattered.

"I could hear Kat crying nearby. When I looked around, I saw a half-dozen empty beer bottles and realized what must have happened. Kat stood there looking frightened and guilty, and I'm ashamed to say I saw red and started yelling at her.

"I'd jumped to the wrong conclusion. I blamed her for bringing the alcohol, when in fact a couple of seniors from the high school were the culprits. They'd gone off to buy more.

"And as if that wasn't bad enough, I realized Kat had pulled Piper out of the water and saved her life. Unfortunately I never got the chance to apologize for all the things I said."

Kate sat stunned at Marsh's emotional outpouring. For a moment she wondered if she wasn't dreaming, but she could feel the faint breeze tugging at her hair and hear the bees buzzing nearby.

The urge to tell him she was Kat, the woman he'd been talking about, was overwhelming.

"Marsh…" she began tentatively, not really sure where to begin. "There's something—"

Before she could say more, her words were cut off by a terrified scream. Startled, Kate turned in time to see Sabrina, her expression one of fear, running toward them.

Chapter Nine

Marsh cursed under his breath and shifted onto his knees. If anything happened to Sabrina...it didn't bear thinking about. He could hear his daughter crying, and not for the first time, anger, frustration and a feeling of helplessness washed over him.

"There's no blood or broken bones," he heard Kate say in a calm voice.

Relief flooded through him. "Sabrina, sweetheart, what happened?"

"Daddy, I was scared!"

Before Marsh could reply, he was suddenly hit full force by what he quickly realized was his daughter. As her arms went around his neck, he struggled to retain his balance.

"Hey, it's all right, I've got you," he soothed, hugging her to him, amazed that she'd actually sought solace in his arms. "What scared you?"

Sabrina hiccuped and drew away. "I was just playing in the water when something wiggled over my foot. I thought it was a snake, like the one in the book Kate read to me yesterday."

"Aw…sweetie, there are no snakes in the lake." As Marsh continued to hold her, it dawned on him that this was the first time his daughter had lowered the barriers to let him in. Feelings of love and gratitude engulfed him, making him forget everything but the child in his arms. He inhaled, drawing in her sweet scent, savoring this precious moment.

"It was probably a leafy plant or a little tadpole swimming by," Kate offered the explanation.

She'd been surprised when Sabrina launched herself into her father's arms, but the look on Marsh's face told its own story. Father and daughter had just made another major breakthrough.

"I thought something was biting my toes. I was scared."

"I'd have been scared, too," Marsh replied, stroking a hand down his daughter's hair. "Hey…I'll tell you what. Why don't I kiss your toes better? Isn't that what daddies are supposed to do. Kiss all the hurts away?"

Sabrina giggled. The sound curled around his heart.

"But Daddy, you can't see my toes."

"You're absolutely right. I'm pretty sure I could find them, though." He caught a handful of her hair in his hand. "This is your toe, right?"

Sabrina's laughter, bubbly and infectious, echoed around him. He smiled.

"Daddy, that's not my toes, that's my hair," she told him, still laughing.

"I knew that. Wait…I think I've got it right this time. I've found your toes." Marsh tugged at her ear.

Sabrina squealed in delight at her father's silly antics.

From her seat on the edge of the blanket, Kate smiled as she watched Marsh charm his daughter. She longed to join in their laughter, be a part of their family, but she knew it was a foolish fantasy. She was only hired help.

Her thoughts shifted to those moments when he'd expressed his regret at not having had the chance to apologize to her.

But while Marsh might have some residual feelings of guilt about the way he'd treated her that summer, they were simply a reflection of his personal sense of decency and justice, nothing more.

"I think it's time we headed home," Marsh said a few minutes later.

"Can we come back and have a picnic another day, Daddy?"

"We sure can. Now, why don't you give Kate a hand to clean up, then you can lead me to the car."

Sabrina happily did as her father asked.

Kate was silent throughout the drive to the ranch house. Bringing the car to a halt in front of the house, she turned off the engine and climbed out to feel the hot, afternoon sun.

"Well, it's about time somebody showed up around here." The deep resonant voice came from the veranda.

Kate threw a startled glance at the man standing at the top of the stairs. Dressed in blue jeans, a crisp white T-shirt, with rugged features and hair streaked with gold, Kate judged him to be an inch taller than Marsh's six feet—but not as handsome.

"Spencer! Darn it all. Why didn't you call and tell us you were coming?" Marsh said as he eased himself out of the back seat of the car.

"I wasn't sure I'd make the flight connection from L.A.," Spencer replied as he sauntered down the stairs toward them.

"Daddy? Who's that?" Sabrina asked, standing next to her father.

"That's your uncle Spencer," Marsh replied.

"Hi, Sabrina," Spencer greeted his niece with a friendly smile. "My, but you've grown. The last time I saw you, you were just a little baby."

"I was?" Sabrina said, her eyes wide.

"You sure were," Spencer replied, still smiling. "I bet you're big enough to give your old uncle a hug," he said. "What do you say?" Spencer crouched down and opened his arms.

Sabrina shyly lowered her head.

"Sabrina's the best hugger in town," Marsh said.

Spencer, who had reached his niece, bent to scoop her into his arms. "Your daddy says you're the best hugger. Can you show me?" he asked, his smile warm and friendly.

Sabrina, obviously charmed by her uncle, quickly gave him the hug he'd asked for.

"Marsh, you're absolutely right. She is the best hugger." He turned to Kate. "You must be the nurse I talked to...."

"Yes. I'm Kate, Kate Turner," she responded, flashing him a polite smile, safe in the knowledge that Spencer wouldn't recognize her since he'd been traveling in Europe when she'd visited before.

"It's a pleasure to meet you, Kate. I hope my brother isn't proving to be too difficult. They say doctors make the worst patients, and he has a tendency to be bossy, to boot," he added, humor evident in his voice.

"Ha! You have no need to worry about Kate," Marsh said. "Believe me, she's quite capable of looking out for herself."

At Marsh's comment, Kate felt her face grow warm. "It's a pleasure to meet you, Mr. Diamond," she said, hoping Spencer wouldn't notice the color rising in her cheeks.

Spencer's slow smile brought a twinkle to his blue eyes. "Mr. Diamond is my father. Please call me Spencer."

"Uncle Spencer?"

"Yes, princess."

"Princess! I'm not a princess!"

"Well you sure look like a princess to me. That'll be my special nickname for you. All right?"

"There's lemonade in the fridge," Kate said. "Why don't we all go inside and have some."

"Lemonade sounds like a good idea to me," Spencer said as he lowered Sabrina to the ground.

Kate automatically moved to Marsh's side and led him to the kitchen.

"So what brings you home early, big brother?" Marsh asked as he curled his hands around the glass Kate had set at his fingertips.

"Queenie. She's about ready to foal, and I wanted to be here."

"Who's Queenie?" Sabrina asked.

"Queenie is one of my favorite mares. Queenie is her nickname."

"Like princess is mine," Sabrina said, sounding pleased.

"That's right!"

"But why did you give a horse a nickname?" she asked curling up her nose a little in distaste.

"Don't you like horses?"

Sabrina shook her head. "I don't think so."

"Sabrina hasn't grown up around horses the way we did."

"I see. Well, she'll soon find out how much fun horses are. And once Queenie's foal is born, perhaps you can come down to the stables and see it."

Sabrina glanced at her father, then at Kate. She could see the look of indecision in the child's eyes as well as a flicker of interest.

"I'll go to the stables with you, if you like." Marsh spoke casually, undoubtedly reading lack of interest into his daughter's silence.

"Would you really, Daddy?" Surprise and pleasure echoed through Sabrina's voice.

"Of course! And who knows, maybe by then

I'll be able to see the foal,'' he added, his tone bright and optimistic.

''Okay! When will the baby foal get borned?''

Kate watched a smile spread across Marsh's features. Her pulse jerked crazily in response, and a longing assailed her. She turned to find Spencer watching her, a look of speculation in his eyes.

''I think it's time I started making dinner.'' Kate spun away from the table.

As she left the room, a pain stabbed at her heart. With Spencer's return, it was only a matter of time before she would no longer be needed.

''So, Kate. Are you from around here?'' Spencer asked as he pushed his empty plate aside and leaned back in his chair. Marsh had insisted that they all eat in the dining room.

Kate brought her water glass to her lips and swallowed several mouthfuls before answering. ''No, I'm not,'' she answered quietly.

''Where are you from?''

''The Los Angeles area. What were you doing over in Ireland?'' she asked, attempting to shift the conversation away from her.

''Looking at racehorses.''

''Is the countryside as beautiful and green as the pictures I've seen?''

''Very much so. But, tell me where—''

"Would you like coffee?" she asked, determined to derail him from his quest to find out more about her.

"Not right now, thank you. The pork chops were delicious, by the way—"

"Thank you. Excuse me, I'll clear away the dishes and check on the coffee." She pushed back her chair, gathered up several empty plates and headed to the kitchen.

"Kate doesn't like to talk about herself," Spencer commented.

"It would seem that way," Marsh replied. He'd been thinking the same thing while he listened to Kate sidestep his brother's questions. "I've been wondering...how old do you think she is?"

"My guess would be twenty-five or six. And she's very attractive, in case you were wondering that, too," he added, humor lacing his voice.

"Kate's got pretty hair," Sabrina piped up. "It's long and brown and has curls like mine. She ties it back with a ribbon sometimes."

"I'd say her eyes are her most interesting feature," Spencer commented. "They're green, and though I might be off base, I'd say there's a sad—" He broke off abruptly, and Marsh knew instantly that Kate had returned.

Spencer made no more attempts to draw Kate out, and as Marsh sat listening to his brother shift from one topic to another, he began to conjure up an image of Kate in his mind.

He pictured her with a heart-shaped face and shoulder-length brown hair tied back in a ribbon as Sabrina had described. Green eyes, a button nose and a generous mouth.

After everything she'd done for him in the past week, he knew her to be a woman of strength and character. A smile tugged at his mouth as he recalled how she'd taken him to task for his childish behavior.

She was also kind and loving, warm and patient, treating Sabrina like her own daughter. He couldn't recall ever knowing anyone like her, and she was a far cry from Tiffany, the self-centered, self-indulgent woman he'd married.

He tried to focus on the image floating inside his head. There was something familiar…she reminded him a little of Kat, but perhaps that was simply because he'd been talking about Kat earlier.

"You know bro…once you get your sight back and start your new job at the hospital, we're going to need a housekeeper."

"That's true."

"We should ask Kate if she'd like the job on a permanent basis. What do you say, Kate? Are you interested?"

"Thank you, but I already have a job."

"Really! Where?"

"In the hospital's new wing. I start the beginning of September."

"Good, that gives us time to change your mind," Spencer countered. "Are you open to bribery?"

Kate laughed aloud.

The soft melodic sound caught Marsh totally off guard. There was something decidedly familiar about the quick, spontaneous sound, something he couldn't quite put his finger on.

Suddenly, somewhere in the depths of his mind, a vague, unformulated memory stirred. Had he met Kate before? That was definitely the feeling he was getting, a feeling that grew stronger with each passing minute.

Kate was a nurse, and it was entirely possible he'd worked with her, perhaps even in Chicago. But surely she would have mentioned the fact. And if not, why not?

Marsh frowned. He wished Spencer had managed to get Kate to talk, to reveal something about herself that might give him a clue. Her name, Kate Turner, didn't ring any bells.

Kate's musical laughter rang out again, and this time Marsh was convinced he'd heard the sound before.

Sipping his coffee, Marsh listened to his brother chatting to Kate and Sabrina. Spencer was talking about his trip to Ireland and telling an amusing tale about one of the horses he'd been hoping to buy.

Sabrina's laughter joined Kate's and for a moment Marsh wondered if Spencer was deliberately flirting with Kate. He had said she was very attractive. Marsh frowned, disturbed more than he cared to admit by the notion.

Kate... It surprised him how often she kept popping into his mind, Marsh thought later that night as he lay tossing around in his bed.

The house had been quiet for several hours, but he'd been too restless to sleep.

Sighing, he set his feet on the floor and stood up. He ran his hand down the bed and located his pants. Though he was becoming more accustomed to his world of darkness, it took some time to get dressed and find his way downstairs and into the kitchen.

Upstairs in Piper's room, Kate closed the book she'd been reading. She was sure she'd heard something. Unable to sleep, she'd opted to read for a while and after browsing Piper's bookshelves, had chosen an old favorite, *Pride and Prejudice*.

She loved the proud, brooding character of Mr. Darcy, who she quickly realized reminded her more than a little of Marsh, especially when they'd first arrived at the ranch after his release from the hospital.

Marsh had been frustrated and angry because of his blindness. Mr. Darcy, on the other hand, had been upset for a very different reason. He hadn't liked the fact that he was attracted to the strong-willed and lovely Miss Elizabeth Bennet, a woman beneath his standing.

A dull thud jolted Kate from her musings, confirming her suspicion that someone was downstairs. It was probably Spencer. After helping her clear the supper dishes, he'd gone down to the stables to check on Queenie, the mare who was ready to foal. Perhaps something was wrong. Maybe she could help.

Pushing the covers aside, she slid her feet into her slippers, grabbed her cotton housecoat off the bed and headed for the door. Switching on the hall lights, she hurried down the stairs. At the bottom she hesitated, wondering if this was a good idea after all.

Suddenly she heard a muffled curse coming from the kitchen, followed by a loud clatter.

Kate ran to the kitchen and switched on the light. To her astonishment she saw Marsh sprawled on the floor with one of the chairs upended beside him.

"Marsh! What happened?" Kate moved the chair out of harm's way and crouched beside him, fearful he'd injured himself in the fall.

"Tripped over the blasted chair," Marsh muttered pulling himself into a sitting position.

"Are you hurt?"

"Only my ego," he replied gruffly.

Kate smiled. "What are you doing down here, anyway? All you had to do was knock on my door or call out if you wanted something."

Marsh shifted and tried to get to his feet. "The house was quiet. I thought everyone was asleep. I didn't want to wake you."

"Here, let me help you up."

Kate helped Marsh to his feet, all too aware that he was naked from the waist up. Her gaze was drawn to the smattering of dark hairs on his broad chest, and suddenly her fingers itched to stroke and explore the muscular contours of his body.

Annoyed at the lustful route her thoughts had taken, she released him and took a step back—only to collide with the chair he'd tripped over. Startled, she lurched forward bumping hard against Marsh. With her senses already in overdrive, she gasped at the unexpected contact that sent tiny electric shocks reverberating through her.

"Hey!" Marsh said, surprise in his voice, as his hands came up to grasp her upper arms. "Are you okay?"

Kate's breath locked in her throat. She could feel his warm breath on her forehead, smell the dark masculine scent that was his alone. She willed herself to move to break free of his hold, but her feet seemed to be glued to the floor.

"Kate?" Her name was a whisper of sound, sending a shiver through her, stirring her senses and awakening needs she'd learned to ignore.

The tension vibrating between them was like a living, breathing entity, Marsh thought. The scent of jasmine swarmed his senses, and the feel of Kate's body brushing against his was like drawing a match across sandpaper.

His hands tightened their hold, and with unerring accuracy he lowered his mouth to hers. The explosion of heat and need that catapulted through him was like nothing he'd ever known before.

Her lips parted beneath his, whether in surprise or invitation he wasn't exactly sure, but he didn't stop to ask. With his tongue he began to make urgent forays into the moist depths of her mouth. When he felt her tongue entwine with his in what quickly became an erotic dance, desire slammed into him, bringing him to full arousal.

Sliding his hands up and over her shoulders, he quickly became entangled in the silky softness of her hair. He couldn't seem to get enough of her, the taste, the scent, the feel of her.

He wanted her. Here! Now! And he didn't need to see her to know she wanted him, too. Above the roar of blood rushing through him he could hear their hearts beating in unison. He'd never felt more alive. He drew her closer, wanting her to know exactly what effect she was having on him.

She moaned into his mouth, and Marsh was sure that if he didn't have her soon, he'd explode.

Suddenly the back door opened. "Oh! Sorry!"

At the sound of Spencer's voice, Kate instantly broke free of Marsh's embrace.

"Kate…" Marsh reached for her, but she dodged out of his reach.

"I'm sorry," she mumbled, and before Marsh could respond he heard the sound of footsteps running down the tiled hallway.

Chapter Ten

Marsh had kissed her! He'd actually kissed her! It hadn't been a dream. Kate's body was still trembling from the aftershock, reminding her just how much she'd wanted him, still wanted him.

Once she reached Piper's bedroom and had closed the door, she brought her fingers to her lips. She could still feel the imprint of his mouth on hers, taste the heady passion that had exploded between them like a firecracker on the Fourth of July.

The need he'd aroused hovered just beneath the surface, leaving her edgy and aching for release. The sheer intensity of the desire that had spiraled through her had rocked her to the core. She'd never felt so alive before, nor had she experienced the depth of emotion he'd ignited with just a kiss.

She'd wanted him quite desperately, and when he'd pulled her close and deepened the kiss, she'd quickly been made aware of how much he'd wanted her.

At the memory of those moments her heart picked up speed once more. Pressing her hand to her chest, she willed it to slow down to a normal pace.

How was she going to face him in the morning? Her thoughts came to an abrupt halt, and she almost laughed aloud at her own foolishness. Marsh wouldn't be able to see her cheeks as they grew hot with embarrassment, or notice the longing she felt sure would be evident in her eyes.

Shrugging out of her housecoat, Kate crossed to the bed and climbed beneath the sheets. What would have happened if Spencer hadn't appeared? Would Marsh have made love to her?

"Kate! Are you awake yet?" Sabrina asked, her tone tentative.

Kate fought her way out of the realms of sleep and rolled over. She opened her eyes to see Sabrina standing by her bedside, dressed in pink shorts and a matching short-sleeved blouse.

"Sabrina! What are you doing here?" Kate sat bolt upright. Surely she hadn't overslept?

"I've been awake for ages," Sabrina said.

"Daddy's awake, too. He told me not to 'sturb you."

"So why are you disturbing Kate?" Marsh asked.

The sound of his deep, resonant voice caused Kate's heart to do a complete somersault. She darted a glance past Sabrina to where he stood in the doorway.

He wore a pair of denim cutoffs and a navy T-shirt. His casual attire added a rugged and relaxed quality to his appearance she found appealing.

His hair was still wet from the shower. He'd attempted to brush it into some semblance of order, but the result was a somewhat disheveled, yet utterly enticing look. Several dark strands curled invitingly over his forehead, hiding the scar that was healing well. The bruising around his eyes had faded, and he looked incredibly sexy and decidedly male.

"It's all right, Sabrina. I'm glad you woke me. I guess I must have slept through the radio alarm. I'm sorry." Kate pushed the covers aside.

"Sabrina, let's go downstairs and give Kate a chance to get dressed. If you're willing to help, we might manage to pour ourselves a glass of orange juice."

"Okay," Sabrina said and, flashing Kate a smile, ran toward her father.

The minute Sabrina and Marsh departed, Kate headed for the bathroom. After a quick shower she pulled on a pair of white shorts and a sleeveless floral blouse. Tying her hair back, she deftly twisted it into a knot at her nape.

"Who'd like pancakes? Or what about egg on toast?" she asked cheerfully when she joined them in the kitchen.

"Pancakes!" Sabrina replied. "I love pancakes."

"Me, too!" Marsh agreed cheerily from his seat at the table.

"Pancakes it is." Kate opened a cupboard door and extracted a large bowl. Reaching for the canister of whole wheat flour, she began to gather the dry ingredients and start the coffeemaker.

As she worked, she told herself she should be relieved that there was no awkwardness or tension in the air. But instead she felt disappointed and faintly annoyed that Marsh appeared to have forgotten their electrifying kiss.

"Good morning." Spencer greeted them as he entered the kitchen through the back door.

Kate felt the heat of embarrassment rush to her cheeks, recalling how he'd walked in last night to find her in Marsh's arms.

"What a night, what a morning, what a beautiful day," Spencer said. "Is the coffee on?"

"Uh...good morning. Coffee's on, but it isn't ready."

Spencer looked weary and rather bedraggled, almost as if he'd spent the night in a hayloft. Suddenly Kate remembered the imminent arrival of the new foal.

"Queenie! Did she have her foal?" Kate asked, feeling sure it was the reason for Spencer's disheveled appearance.

"She has indeed. At around five this morning."

"That's terrific," Marsh said. "Colt or filly?"

"Colt. And believe me, he's a beaut. He's got winner stamped all over him. Who'd like to come down to the stables with me after breakfast and see the new foal?"

"I'd love to see the foal," Kate said.

"Why don't we all go to the stables?" Marsh suggested.

After finishing breakfast, the small procession headed down the shaded pathway to the stables. Spencer and Sabrina led the way, while Kate and Marsh brought up the rear.

The moment Marsh had slipped his hand beneath Kate's elbow, his touch sent a jolt of electricity through her. She barely managed to quell the impulse to break free, as her senses scrambled and the ache she'd been ignoring since she woke returned in full force.

Silently she reminded herself that the kiss they'd shared had been a mistake, a mistake she didn't regret, but a mistake she couldn't afford to let happen again.

As Marsh walked a half step behind Kate, he could feel the tension emanating from her. He was sure she was also thinking back to the kiss they'd shared.

The urge to stop and pull her into his arms and taste again the erotic flavor of her mouth was almost overwhelming.

And more than ever he wished he could gaze into Kate's eyes to see for himself if she'd been as affected by the kiss as he'd been. If she'd wanted him as intensely as he'd wanted her...still wanted her.

His instant and mind-blowing response had had all the power behind it of a nuclear explosion. And he couldn't recall ever experiencing such a strong and driving need to possess her. She'd quite simply annihilated his control, and the speed and urgency of the desire she'd aroused in him had left him reeling.

If Spencer hadn't chosen that exact moment to

arrive, he'd have made love to Kate right there on the kitchen table.

But Spencer had appeared, and as a result Marsh had spent the night in torment and frustration. He was still edgy, and it had taken not a little effort on his part to act as if nothing had happened.

He wasn't sure exactly how or when it had happened, but Kate, with quiet persistence and unending patience, had been slowly chipping away at the ice around his heart.

"Kate, I owe you an apology." Marsh's voice was husky, and the words sent a chill through her.

"For what?" she asked, keeping her tone even, though she knew exactly what he was talking about.

"For the way I behaved last night. I was out of line. I'm sorry."

He was sorry he'd kissed her. Pain stabbed at her heart, but she ignored it. "It was only a kiss," she said, pretending indifference. "Apology accepted," she added, though her heart was slowly breaking.

Marsh's steps faltered, and the toe of his shoe caught, pitching him forward.

Kate reacted quickly, instantly putting herself in his path. She inhaled sharply as Marsh bumped against her, and for the second time in as many days she suddenly found herself pressed intimately against him.

Heat sprinted through her, leaving a trail of need in its wake. He was too close for comfort. His mouth only inches away, and it was all she could do not to close the gap between them.

She tried to take a step back, but his arms held her fast. Tension arced between them like a living, breathing thing.

"Thanks. I'd have been a goner for sure." His breath fanned her face, sending a shiver of desire snaking through her.

"No problem," she replied, hoping he wouldn't hear the slight waver in her voice or the frantic pounding of her heart.

As they approached the security fence, Kate could see that the yard and buildings had grown considerably from what she remembered. Spencer punched in the security code and opened the gate.

"We moved Queenie into this stable block before I went to Ireland. This is where we keep the family's riding horses. It's much quieter," Spencer explained as Kate led Marsh through the gate.

The stable was open and airy, with eight stalls, four on each side.

"Queenie is in one of the bigger stalls at the end of the row," Spencer said as they made their way past the stalls. Several heads poked out over the doors, and Kate glanced at Sabrina who was gazing around in obvious interest.

"If you'd like to wait here for a minute, I'll take a peek and see how mother and son are doing." Without waiting for a reply he strode off.

The familiar smell of horses, hay and feed enveloped them. Kate smiled as happy memories resurfaced.

Nearby a horse snorted and shook his head.

Sabrina had darted to her father's side, putting her hand in his. "Daddy, I'm scared."

"There's nothing to be scared about," Marsh assured her. "Want me to pick you up?"

"Yes, please."

Marsh released his hold on Kate and carefully crouched down. He gathered her into his arms and stood up.

"Now tell me, what do you see that frightens you?"

"A...a big horse. He's looking at me."

"Is he showing you his teeth and trying to bite you?"

Sabrina giggled a little nervously. "No, he's nodding his head and making funny snuffling noises," she told him.

"He's sniffing the air trying to catch your scent. He's curious that's all. He hasn't seen many pretty little girls like you before," her father said teasingly. "What color is he?"

"Brown with a little white spot on his nose," Sabrina said, beginning to sound less fearful.

"Their names are usually on the stall door. Kate, what's the horse's name?"

"Primrose. Her name's Primrose." She'd been staring at the name, sure it must be a mistake. Primrose had been the name of the horse she'd learned to ride, the mare Marsh had assured her was as gentle as a lamb. He'd been right.

"Primrose! Well, she's an old friend," Marsh said, affection in his voice. "Primrose is your grandmother's favorite horse, she's sweet-natured and very gentle. Hey, Primrose, old girl. How are you?"

Primrose whinnied softly in response to the low rumble of his voice.

"She's saying hello," Marsh said.

"Everything's fine. Come and see our new addition," Spencer said as he rejoined them.

Kate quickly moved to Marsh's side. He lowered Sabrina to the ground. With an eagerness that surprised Kate, Sabrina ran to her uncle's side. Together they walked to the stall.

"Remember to stay quiet and not frighten him," Spencer cautioned. "Sabrina, you'll see him much better if I lift you up."

Spencer bent to scoop Sabrina into his arms. The minute she spotted the tiny foal standing next to his mother, her mouth rounded in wonder and her eyes became as big as saucers. "Oh, look! He's so pretty!" Sabrina said as Spencer put her back down. "Daddy! Look!" Sabrina invited, turning to smile at her father, a smile Kate only wished he could see.

"I wish I could," Marsh replied, but there was no anger or bitterness in his voice.

Kate caught the glint of moisture in Marsh's eyes and felt her heart contract.

During the past few days he'd made a supreme effort to put his own problems on the back burner and concentrate instead on his daughter and their relationship. The strategy appeared to be paying dividends.

Sabrina was a warm, loving child, eager to please, and the attention and love her father had been showering on her had set their relationship on a new course.

"He's adorable," Kate acknowledged enthusiastically, admiring the foal's chestnut coloring and the blaze of white on his forehead.

"The whole family's come out to admire the new addition, I see." The comment came from behind them.

"Kyle, I didn't know you were still here,"

Spencer turned to greet the man who'd joined them.

"I thought I'd take a quick look before I go."

"You remember my brother, Marsh," Spencer said. "And this pretty little lady is his daughter, Sabrina, and the other pretty lady is Kate Turner. This is Kyle Masters, our local veterinarian."

"Kate Turner," Kyle went on, turning to look at Kate. "I don't know why, but that name sounds familiar," he said flashing her a friendly smile. "Have we met before?"

Kate's heart jammed against her rib cage. He obviously didn't recognize her. For that she was immensely relieved.

"No, I don't think so," Kate said. She met Kyle Masters's gaze, thinking he'd filled out considerably since she'd last seen him. She wondered if Piper, who'd had a crush on him, had ever managed to catch his eye.

"It's a common enough name, I suppose," Kate continued lightly. "Your work as a vet must be very rewarding, especially when you see results like this beautiful colt," she went on, intent on diverting attention away from herself.

"You've got that right."

"This is the first time Sabrina has ever been near a horse," Spencer said.

"Would you like to go inside the stall and pat the foal?" Kyle asked.

Sabrina's gaze was riveted on Kyle. "Can I?" she asked breathlessly.

"It's fine with me," Marsh said, wishing he were the one taking her, but pleased all the same that she sounded excited at the prospect.

"I'll go with you," Spencer offered.

Marsh was thrilled by Sabrina's willingness to enter the stable, pleased that like most children her innate curiosity about life had overcome her initial fear.

During the past few days, his relationship with Sabrina had undergone a dramatic change, and he knew he had Kate to thank for the progress they'd made. Sabrina was becoming deeply attached to Kate and no doubt she'd be upset when the time came for Kate to leave. Suddenly Marsh acknowledged that Sabrina wouldn't be the only one who wasn't looking forward to Kate's departure.

From another stall, Marsh heard and recognized Primrose's nicker and heard too the faint murmur of Kate's voice. Using his hands to feel his way along the stall, he moved quietly toward them.

"We had such good times, didn't we girl," she was saying. "You were the most patient and sweetest horse in the world." Affection laced her voice. "You, lovely lady, and Marsh and Piper all deserve credit for teaching me to ride."

Marsh frowned. What on earth could she be talking about? Unless... She was Kat! Kate Turner was his sister's old school friend!

Why hadn't he recognized her name? Because he'd only ever known her as Kat. That's how Piper had introduced her. Marsh remembered thinking how appropriate the nickname was for the brown-haired beauty with the haunting green eyes.

He hadn't known Kat was Sam Rawlins's daughter until he heard his father firing Rawlins for being drunk on the job the day Piper had nearly drowned.

No wonder Kate had been reluctant to talk about her past, and hesitant when he'd offered her the job. The last time they met he'd lambasted her for her irresponsible behavior, practically accusing her of causing Piper's accident. He could only speculate that the fact he couldn't see her was more than likely the only reason she'd agreed to help him.

Feelings of regret and shame washed over him. He'd lashed out at her without thinking, and the guilt he'd felt had weighed on his mind for a very long time. He could still recall the crushed look in her beautiful green eyes.

He owed her so much. He had to make amends before she walked out of his life a second time.

Chapter Eleven

"**K**ate, we need to talk," Marsh said.

Since their return from the stables, he hadn't been able to get her alone to confirm his suspicion that she was indeed Kat. Sabrina had monopolized his attention, intent on finding out everything about the pony he'd had as a child, and how much care it had required. Kate had busied herself making lunch. But when she'd sent Sabrina to her room in search of a book about horses she'd seen on the shelves, Marsh had seized the opportunity to talk to her.

"Is there anything wrong?" Kate asked, surprised by his serious tone. She set the platter of ham, cheese and tomato sandwiches on the table and returned to the counter for plates and napkins.

"No, of course not. It's just that I wanted to ask…"

"I found it!" Sabrina announced, returning to the kitchen.

"We'll look at it after lunch," Kate said.

"Did I hear someone say lunch?" Spencer asked as he came through the back door.

"Your timing is perfect," Kate commented with a grin.

For the remainder of the day Marsh's attempts to spend a few minutes alone with Kate continued to be thwarted. Silently he resigned himself to waiting until after Sabrina had gone to bed.

As soon as dinner was finished that evening, Kate heard Sabrina running down the hall into her room. She dried her hands and turned to leave the kitchen. To her surprise, she collided with Marsh, who'd appeared directly behind her.

"Oh…sorry. I didn't hear you." Kate said automatically reaching out to steady him. Marsh reacted, too, but being unable to see her, or accurately gauge her location, she felt his hand accidentally brush her breast.

Her gasp of reaction was followed by a powerful jolt of awareness. Dizziness assailed her, along with an ache that was fast becoming familiar and had everything to do with Marsh's presence.

"Did I hurt you? I'm sorry," Marsh sounded distressed, his face a picture of anxiety.

"I'm fine. You just startled me," she said, trying to ignore the way her heart was wobbling crazily inside her chest.

Silence stretched awkwardly between them for several seconds.

"Are you sure you can manage…"

"Of course. I'm making up for lost time. The last few days have been magical. Sabrina and I are making great inroads, and I have you to thank for it."

"I steered you in the right direction, that's all," Kate said modestly, warmed by his words all the same. "I'd better get the kitchen cleaned up." She started to move past him.

"I still want to have that talk."

"Sure," Kate replied, wondering if the reason he wanted to talk was to tell her he no longer needed her services. Pain sliced through her at the thought, but she knew it was a reality she had to face.

Kate returned to the kitchen and loaded the dishwasher. Retrieving the broom from the closet, she began to sweep the tiled floor.

Suddenly the singsong chime of the doorbell echoed through the house. Frowning, she set the broom aside.

When she opened the front door she came face-to-face with a man and a woman. The man appeared to be in his sixties and wore blue jeans, a checkered shirt and a cowboy hat. The woman was at least ten years younger, with blond hair swept up into a French roll. She wore a pair of tight-fitting jeans and a bright red v-necked top.

"Hello," Kate said with a smile.

"Who are you?" the woman asked.

"I...ah, work here," Kate replied.

The woman swept past Kate into the foyer. Her husband followed, but not before flashing Kate an apologetic smile.

"Would you tell Spencer that Genevieve and Raymond Springer are here," the woman said haughtily.

"I'd be happy to," Kate said. Closing the door, she turned and headed for the stairs. She was only partway up when the woman spoke, this time to her husband.

"She must be the new housekeeper. Can't say I'm impressed. Mind you, good help is so hard to find these days."

Kate continued up the stairs, silently pondering the woman's rudeness. Marsh stood on the landing. He'd heard the doorbell, and curiosity had brought him to the top of the stairs. The creak of the stairs and the familiar scent of jasmine teasing his nostrils told him Kate was approaching.

"The Springers are here," he said softly, so as not to be overheard. "It's funny how some people's mindsets never change."

"It would seem that way."

"Once you've told Spencer about his guests, would you stop by my room, I still want to have that talk."

"Yes, of course," Kate replied, her heart already sinking.

As Spencer headed down the stairs, Kate made a stop in Sabrina's room. The little girl was fast asleep, her arms around the teddy bear she'd been hugging the first time Kate had seen her in the hospital.

It seemed like eons ago, but in fact only a little more than a week had passed, a week in which Kate had found herself part of the Diamond family again.

She leaned over to kiss Sabrina's cheek. She was going to miss her terribly—Marsh, too, for that matter. Tears stung her eyes.

If only... The words danced in her head like bees around a honey pot but she shooed them away.

There was no *if only*. She'd been hired to do a job. She was staff, nothing more. And according to Genevieve Springer, not up to standard. She would do well to remember it.

With a sigh Kate rose and left Sabrina's room. She came to a halt outside Marsh's door. Bracing herself for what she felt sure would be her dismissal, she knocked.

"Come in!"

"You wanted to talk to me."

"Yes." Marsh was sitting in the easy chair, the same chair he'd been in when she'd lectured him about neglecting his daughter. Gone were the hunched shoulders and dejected expression. In their place was a more confident man, a man willing to face the daily challenge of being blind.

"I suppose you want to let me go," Kate said simply, needing to get it over with. But at her words a look of surprise appeared on Marsh's face.

"You thought I was going to let you go?"

"Yes. With Spencer back from Ireland you don't really need me...."

"Good grief, Kate, when it comes to looking after himself, Spencer is even worse than I am. We'd never survive without you. No, it isn't that...." He stopped. "I heard you talking to Primrose this morning."

"What?" Kate's heart fluttered against her breast in alarm.

"I thought there was something about you,

something familiar. Are you Kat?" he asked abruptly. "Are you my sister's friend from ten years ago...the one she called Kat?"

Kate was silent for a moment before answering. "Yes, I'm Kat."

"Why didn't you tell me at the hospital?" Marsh asked, annoyance coloring his tone.

Kate bristled. "As I recall, our last meeting wasn't altogether a pleasant one."

"You're right. Listen, Kate, I owe you an apology. Needless to say, it's long overdue. All I can say in my defense is that it wasn't until the next morning, when Piper explained the truth about that night at the lake, that I learned what happened."

"You could have asked me."

Marsh nodded. "You're right, I could have. I should have. But I was so angry and so scared, I wasn't thinking straight. When Piper told me you'd hauled her out of the water, I realized what a fool I'd been. You saved her life, not me."

"That's not true. Yes, I hauled her out of the water, but I had no clue what to do after that. I didn't know how to perform mouth-to-mouth, or CPR. If you hadn't come along when you did—" She broke off unable to continue.

"I tried to find you," Marsh said after a brief pause.

Kate blinked in surprise. "You did?"

"Piper told me where you lived, and I went there to talk to you, to apologize...but you and your father had already left town."

"You went to the apartment?" Kate repeated, scarcely able to believe what she was hearing.

"I wanted to apologize. I behaved like a prize jerk that night. I'd been wrong to accuse you. I should have known you weren't responsible.... I'm truly sorry for the things I said to you that night."

Kate heard the sincerity in his voice, and her throat closed over with emotion, making it impossible for her to speak.

Silence stretched between them for several moments.

"Kate?" Marsh spoke her name tentatively.

"Apology accepted," she said quickly, overwhelmed by the fact that he'd even offered it.

"You're very generous. I wouldn't blame you if you were still angry with me."

"It was a long time ago."

"You're right. It was a long time ago, but I've never forgiven myself for the way I treated you. I've thought about you a lot over the years, wondering where you were, what you were doing." His tone held regret.

For the second time in as many minutes Kate held her breath. The knowledge that Marsh had actually thought about her sent a shiver chasing down her spine.

"Why did you come back to Kincade?"

"I needed a job, and I saw the ad looking for nurses for the hospital's new wing. So I applied."

"I'm curious. What made you choose nursing as a career? Did it have something to do with Piper's accident?"

He surprised her with his perceptiveness. "As a matter of fact it did. I felt so helpless not knowing what to do to help Piper that night. I decided then and there to become a nurse."

"Why not a doctor?"

"I thought about it. But somehow I just never got around to it," she said, unwilling to confess that she'd been on the verge of applying for medical school when Dan had been brought into the hospital. She'd become so involved with Dan's care that she'd put her own ambition on hold. When Dan asked her to marry him she'd seen it as a chance to make the kind of life she'd always dreamed of.

"It's too bad Piper isn't here. Do you know that for the rest of that summer she never let me forget what a jerk I'd been. I couldn't wait to get back to Chicago," he added with a low laugh.

Kate laughed, too, warmed by the knowledge that her friend had continued to stick up for her.

"You did well for yourself in Chicago." She'd come across his name at different times over the years, including reading about his wedding to socialite Tiffany Buchanan.

"Professionally, that's true. But on a personal level I made a lot of mistakes."

"We all make mistakes," Kate replied, hearing the bitterness in his voice. "The trick is to learn from them."

"Oh, I learned, all right. I learned that my dream of one day having the kind of marriage and family life my parents enjoyed was nothing but a pipe dream. I failed at what's really the most important job of all, being part of a family." He sighed again. "Did you have a dream, Kate?"

Kate swallowed the lump of emotion lodged in her throat. She was still trying to come to terms with the fact that Marsh's dream and her own dream had been exactly the same.

"Yes, I had a dream," Kate replied, wondering what he would think if he knew he'd been a central figure in all her dreams, ever since the first time she'd set eyes on him.

"What was your dream, Kate?" he asked as he rose from the chair.

Kate felt her heart flutter as he took a step toward her. She could have sworn he could see her because he was staring straight at her. She felt her mouth go dry and her skin tingle.

"My dream was a lot like yours," she managed to say, trying to keep her tone even, while her pulse beat rapidly.

"After the way you've helped bridge the gap between Sabrina and me, I'd say you've got what it takes to make your dreams come true," Marsh said.

Kate was suddenly glad he couldn't see her face, or the look of longing she felt sure was in her eyes. She wished with all her heart that she could stay here with Marsh and Sabrina, be part of their lives forever. But that was one dream too many....

"Sometimes dreams just aren't meant to be..." she said huskily.

"I know what you mean. I'd just about given up on dreams." He took another step toward her, and though the temptation to retreat was strong, she didn't move. "Would you like to know what I've been dreaming about lately?"

When his hand reached out and brushed her cheek, her heart shuddered to a standstill. With gentle fingers he traced the outline of her cheek and jaw, sending her pulse soaring, and when his thumb came to rest on her lower lip and he caressed its fullness, she thought her knees might buckle.

"This," he said, his voice little more than a husky whisper. With one bold movement his hand cupped her neck, and unerringly he brought his mouth down on hers.

This time the kiss was agonizingly sweet and deliciously tender. Marsh teased and tasted, tantalized and tormented, driving her to distraction and awakening needs she'd never known before.

She opened her mouth and emitted a low moan of frustration. Marsh instantly accepted the throaty invitation, proceeding to plunder and pillage, ravish and ransack, propelling her ever closer to the edge of reason.

Of their own volition her hands came up to rake through his hair and haul him closer. She couldn't seem to get enough, yet she dared to demand more as she responded with an urgency that left her breathless.

Suddenly Marsh lost his balance, and together they toppled toward the bed. They didn't make it. Marsh bounced off the edge and landed on the floor with Kate on top of him.

Kate quickly rolled off, and saw the grimace of pain on Marsh's face. "Marsh? Are you all right?" Anxiety threaded through her voice.

"My head hurts. It feels as if it's going to explode."

"Sit quietly for a moment, I'll get a cold compress and a couple of painkillers.'' She hurried to the bathroom.

When she returned, Marsh was sitting on the edge of the bed, looking pale and in pain.

''I'll ask Spencer to drive you to the hospital. I'll stay with Sabrina.''

''No, it's not necessary.''

''Marsh you really should—''

''I'm fine. If the headache hasn't gone by morning, you can drive me into town to see Dr. Franklin.''

''Are you sure?''

''Positive,'' he told her. ''Look, Kate, I'm not going to apologize this time for what happened just now.''

''You don't have to. And please don't make more of this than there really is,'' she went on, trying to keep her voice matter-of-fact. ''Patients are often attracted to their doctors or to the nurse looking after them. It isn't unusual. Now, I think you should try to get some sleep.''

''Kate...I—''

''Sleep.''

''We're not finished with this,'' Marsh said, sounding tired. ''Not by a long shot....''

Chapter Twelve

Marsh lay on top of his bed willing the relentless pain throbbing inside his head to stop. He'd never had a headache like this before, and he could only hope that it was a prelude to getting his sight back.

Attempting to distract himself, he turned his thoughts to Kate, to conjuring up a picture of her in his mind.

He remembered vividly the first time that he'd laid eyes on her. Tall and skinny, with chocolate-brown hair that reached past her shoulders, she'd been standing on the veranda wearing a pair of skimpy shorts and a V-necked T-shirt.

He'd been out riding, and the sound of his horse's hooves on the hard ground had drawn her attention. When she'd turned to watch his approach, he'd felt his breath hitch and his heart jam against his chest.

He remembered thinking she could easily have been mistaken for a runway model or a budding movie star. But for all her attributes, her incredible green eyes had entranced him, tugging strangely at his heart. He could see a deep sadness in their depths, and a longing she tried hard to conceal.

When Piper rushed out of the house and greeted him with a surprised yell, he'd jumped down off his horse, Apollo, and braced himself for her usual enthusiastic hug.

"This is my friend Kat," Piper had said. "She's new in town and she's in my class at school."

He'd watched Kat come down the steps, totally unaware of her sexuality. She'd tried to appear uninterested, even bored, but he'd noted the pink tinge in her cheeks and the glint of reluctant admiration in her eyes.

What had knocked him off stride was his own reaction to this girl on the brink of womanhood, this teenager who was the same age as his sister.

His purpose in coming home had been to study for his final exams, but instead he'd put aside his medical books and notes to go swimming and riding with the girls. He'd told himself he was a fool. But there was something indefinable about Kat, something that drew him like a magnet, something he'd never quite been able to forget.

On reflection, his anger at Kat the night of Piper's accident had been way out of proportion. He'd needed a reason to reject her, to sever the strong attraction he felt for the teenager who was his sister's friend. But instead he'd been haunted by the wounded look in her eyes.

Marsh dozed fitfully throughout the night as dreams or memories of Kat drifted in and out of his mind. When he awoke, his head still ached, and he felt as though he hadn't slept a wink.

His tiredness was instantly forgotten the second he opened his eyes and realized the darkness had finally lifted. He could see light! Where yesterday there had been total and complete blackness, today there were shadows and shapes.

His breathing hitched, his heart started to pound as tears of joy and relief stung his eyes. Silently he sent up a prayer of thanks and vowed never to take his sight, his daughter, or his life, for granted again.

His vision was returning, he was sure of it. And as he headed for the bathroom, his first thought was that he'd be able to see Kate, to look again into those tantalizing catlike green eyes and find out if fate had offered him a second chance.

"Good morning!" The sound of Marsh's cheerful voice caught Kate off guard. She turned away from her spot at the stove to look at him.

His face was wreathed in smiles, and her heart skipped a beat in response. In that same instant she knew something had changed.

"'Morning Marsh." Spencer pulled out a chair. "What are you all smiles about?"

"I can see!"

"That's terrific!" Spencer said, reaching over to pat his brother on the back.

"You can really see?" Sabrina gazed up at him in wide-eyed excitement.

"Not clearly. But I can distinguish light and dark, and I can see shapes."

"Marsh! That's wonderful!" Kate said, pinning a smile on her face, while inside her heart was breaking.

"I think I'd better take a trip into town and get Tom to take a look."

"I can drive you to the hospital," Spencer offered. "I'm headed to the bank after breakfast. I'll drop you off on my way and pick you up later."

"Sounds like a plan," Marsh said as he felt for the chair and sat down.

"You'll be able to teach me to ride, now, Daddy. Then I can get a pony."

"You, young lady, have a one-track mind."

When the front-door chimes rang out, everyone was silent for a moment.

"Who could that be?" Spencer asked as he set his coffee cup on the table.

He'd only taken a few steps into the hallway when the sound of his laugh rang out. "Well, I'll be! Look what the cat dragged in," he said stepping back into the kitchen.

"What kind of welcome is that?" A voice demanded. The newcomer halted in the doorway, and Kate instantly recognized her old school friend, Piper.

"Piper?" Marsh said as he turned toward the voice.

"In the flesh. Don't I get a hug from my big brothers?" she demanded, smiling first at Marsh and then at Spencer.

Spencer grabbed his sister and kissed her soundly. When he released her, she crossed to where Marsh stood and hauled him into her arms.

"How are you?" Piper asked, once Marsh let her go.

"Better, much better."

Piper's gaze shifted to Sabrina. "You must be Sabrina! What a cutie! Hi! I'm your aunt," she said, and gently ruffled Sabrina's hair.

"Hi!" Sabrina said, smiling at the newcomer.

Piper's eyes shifted to Kate at the stove. "Hello..." She stopped, and a frown creased her tanned face. "It can't be? Kat! Is it really you? I don't believe it. It's so good to see you."

Kate felt tears prick her eyes at the warmth in Piper's voice. Before she could say anything she found herself wrapped in Piper's warm embrace.

"Hello, Piper," Kate managed to say once her friend stepped back.

"Kat, you haven't changed. You still look like a million bucks!" Piper said. "I'm still mad at you, you know, for disappearing like that without a word. Why didn't you ever write or call? The last time I saw you you saved my life. The least you could have done was stick around so I could thank you."

Kate felt her cheeks grow warm. "I'm sorry. You're right. I should have written..."

"Never mind that now. It's wonderful that you're here. We've got so much to catch up on. What have you been doing with your life? Why are you here?"

Kate laughed. She couldn't help it. Piper hadn't changed either. "Which question do you want me to answer first? Wait—breakfast is getting cold. Sit down. I don't want this food to go to waste."

"Don't mind if I do. The food on the plane was terrible," Piper said as she joined her brothers and niece at the table.

Kate quickly served up the food and filled the coffee cups. She sat and listened to the friendly bantering between Piper and her brothers.

Piper was thrilled when Marsh told her he believed his eyesight was returning. Once the food had been demolished, Piper sat back and smiled.

"It's good to be home," she said.

"Why are you home?" Spencer ventured to ask.

"I knew Mom and Dad were in Ireland, so I flew over for a quick visit with them. When they told me about Marsh's accident I thought I'd come home and see if I could help," she explained. "But it would appear I'm too late."

Spencer glanced at his watch. "Hey, bro...we'd better get going. My appointment's at nine."

"Hey, where are you off to? I just got here!" Piper complained.

"Marsh wants to let Dr. Franklin check his eyes, and I have a meeting with the bank manager," Spencer explained.

"The bank manager. That sounds ominous," Piper teased. "Well, with you two gone it will give me a chance to get to know my niece and to catch up with Kat," she went on.

Once Spencer and Marsh had departed, Piper and Sabrina and Kate cleared away the breakfast dishes.

"Kate, I'm going upstairs to get my horse book to show Piper," Sabrina said.

"She's a cutie," Piper commented after Sabrina scurried off. "My brother has been through a lot lately, more than his share, I'd say. Speaking of

my brother. Do you still have a crush on him?"
Piper asked.

"I never— How did—" Kate broke off. She
glanced at Piper and they both started to laugh.

"It's so good to see you, Kat." Piper said. "After you left, I really missed you, you know. Why
didn't you call or write? You were my best friend.
You saved my life."

Kate shook her head. "Marsh saved your life,"
she said. "And as for calling or writing. Well, I
thought a clean break was best."

"I know what you mean," Piper said, and at the
wistful note in her friend's voice Kate had the impression she was talking about something else entirely.

"How long are you staying?" Kate asked.
"Marsh was telling me you're a freelance photographer, that you travel all over the world. That
must be exciting."

Piper yawned again. "Oh...I'm sorry," she
said. "It must be jet lag. I'm suddenly wiped...."

Kate smiled. "Why don't you go have a nap.
Oh, wait. I've been using your bedroom."

"No problem," Piper said. "I'll go and crash in
my parents' room." She yawned again. "We'll
talk later, okay? Tell Sabrina I'll look at the book
later, too."

Alone now, Kate hugged herself, feeling a sob
rise in her throat. She longed to be a part of this

wonderful family, but the morning's events proved her job here was over.

Her thoughts turned to Marsh and to the kiss they'd shared last night. Her heart wanted to believe that what Marsh felt for her was more than gratitude, but her head kept getting in the way.

A tiny voice reminded her that she was her father's daughter, nothing more than hired help, that she wasn't in the same league and that she didn't belong.

"Kate? Where's Piper?" Sabrina asked when she reappeared carrying several books.

Kate brushed a stray tear from her eye. "She went to lie down and take a nap," she said.

Sabrina frowned. "I wanted to show her the book about horses."

"You can show her later when she wakes up," Kate said.

"Maybe when Daddy and Uncle Spencer get back we can go to the stables and see the foal again," Sabrina said in a hopeful tone.

"Why don't we go and see him right now?"

"Can we?"

Already out the door, Sabrina ran down the steps and across the yard. Kate followed more slowly, and with each step she felt a sadness seep into her bones. After Hank let them in, Sabrina scampered on ahead and quickly climbed up onto a bale of hay to get a better view of inside the stall.

"Oh, Kate, look how he's grown," Sabrina said excitedly. "I'm going to ride him one day."

"I'd like to see that."

"You will."

Kate bit her lip. "I don't think so," she said evenly.

"Why?" Sabrina asked, turning her blue eyes so like her father's to look at Kate.

"Because I won't be here."

"Why not?"

"Because your father's eyesight is coming back, and he only hired me to look after the two of you until he could see again. He doesn't need me anymore."

"You're leaving?" Sabrina's voice wobbled. Kate saw the tears pooling in her eyes.

"Not right this minute," Kate said with a smile. "But soon."

"But you can't go!" Sabrina was on the verge of tears.

"Sweetheart, don't cry," Kate said, her heart breaking. "You'll have your father and Uncle Spencer and Aunt Piper to look after you, and pretty soon your grandparents will be back. You won't even notice I'm gone," she added brightly.

Sabrina was silent this time, and suddenly Kate realized Sabrina wasn't looking at her but looking past her. She turned, and her heart jolted to a standstill when she saw Marsh standing just inside the stable door.

The foal forgotten, Sabrina jumped down from the hay bale and ran to her father. "Daddy! Kate says she's leaving, that we don't need her anymore. You have to make her stay," she pleaded.

Marsh removed the sunglasses Dr. Franklin had told him to wear. He saw the fuzzy image of his daughter running toward him, and he quickly bent down to take her in his arms. "Hey, sweetie, don't cry. We'll sort this out. But first I need to talk to Kate."

"I don't want her to go," Sabrina said, sniffing now.

"I know. Look, why don't you run up to the house. Uncle Spencer has a surprise for you. Off you go," he urged gently as he opened the stable door. "Kate and I will be along shortly."

"I didn't mean to upset her," Kate said. "But my job here is over."

"I suppose you're right," Marsh said. He wished he could see her clearly, but she was too far away.

"What did Dr. Franklin say? Is your sight fully restored?"

"Not quite," Marsh replied as he slowly walked toward her. "But Tom and I are both sure that in the next few days it should be back to normal."

"I'm glad," Kate said, trying to ignore the way

her heart was suddenly hammering against her ribs as if trying to escape.

"That's better. I can see you a little more clearly," Marsh said as he halted in front of her. "Your eyes are even more beautiful than I remember," he said.

Kate blushed, and a shiver of longing chased down her spine. "Now that your sight is coming back, my job here is over. You don't need me anymore," she said, not sure who she was trying to convince.

Marsh's slow smile sent her pulse into overdrive. "That's where you're wrong, Kate. We need you more than ever. In fact, Sabrina and I are going to need you for a long time to come."

Kate swallowed convulsively. What did Marsh mean?

"If you're trying to tell me you're grateful I—" Kate began.

"Yes, I'm grateful!" Marsh said. "Grateful that you put a child's needs first and took the job I offered, when you probably felt more like telling me what I could do with the job.

"Grateful that you refused to let me wallow in self-pity and challenged me to take control of my life again.

"Grateful that you helped me be the father Sabrina deserves and showed me that with love and patience and a little effort on my part I could break down the barriers my daughter had erected.

"Oh, yes, I'm grateful," he repeated. "But what I feel for you is much more than gratitude. You've shown Sabrina and me what being a family is all about. You made it happen. You brought us back together, and that makes you a part of our family. If you leave now, this family wouldn't be the same. We'd be missing its most vital part...you."

Kate stared at him in stunned silence, her throat burning with emotion. The sincerity and warmth she'd heard in his voice overwhelmed her. But surely he wasn't saying what she thought.

"You still don't get it, do you?" Marsh said, frustration edging his voice. He wished he could see her more clearly. But he could see enough.

He brought his hand to her cheek. "What I'm trying not-so-eloquently to say Kate is, I love you, I think I always have.

"I was riding Apollo the very first time I saw you, and you bowled me over. There was something about you, something that touched my heart.

"I should have been studying for my finals, but I didn't care if I passed or failed, all I cared about was spending time with you. But you were sixteen, the same age as my sister, for heaven's sake.

"I told myself I was behaving like a fool, that you were much too young for me. I tried to fight the attraction, but you had me tied up in knots. I couldn't get you out of my mind.

"That's probably why I raged at you the night of Piper's accident. Falling in love with you wasn't part of my plan, and I was simply looking for a way out. That night you gave me one.

"I regretted my outburst. I should have known you couldn't have been responsible for what happened to Piper, but I was too mixed up to see straight.

"I never forgot you, Kate. And my feelings for you have always been there, hiding in my heart. I love you. Shall I show you just how much?"

He didn't wait for an answer but closed the gap between them, bringing his mouth down on hers.

Her response was instant and very gratifying to him, because for half a heartbeat he'd begun to doubt she believed him.

Kate gave herself up to the wonder of being in Marsh's arms. She was reeling from his declaration...scarcely able to believe his words. It had to be a dream, but the most wonderful dream in the world.

Heat and need coursed through her, flaring into a passion that only he could appease. She was fast spinning out of control, but she never wanted it to end, never wanted to leave the haven of his arms.

One of the horses began to neigh. Queenie answered, effectively breaking the spell, bringing them back from the brink.

Marsh drew away, his breathing ragged. "Kate, my love, my heart, much as I want you—and make no mistake, I want you—I think we'd better continue this somewhere more private."

"Marsh, are you sure about this?" Kate asked, her tone tentative, still afraid to believe. "We're from such different backgrounds—my father, he's a drunk, remember?"

"I don't care about your father, Kate. I care about you. I love you. You're the woman I want to spend the rest of my life with, the woman who makes my life complete. I want you to be my wife, to be a mother to Sabrina and to any other children that come along." He stopped, out of breath.

"Marsh you don't know how much it means to hear you say that…but—"

"No buts. There can't be any buts, Kate. Unless of course you don't love me…." His words trailed off, hinting of pain, of sadness.

"Of course, I love you!" Kate blurted out, astonished that he could even think she didn't. "I fell in love with you the first moment I saw you riding up on Apollo."

Suddenly Kate's feet were no longer on the ground. Marsh had picked her up and he was spinning her around.

"I was about to give up hope that you'd ever

say it,'' Marsh said when he slowed to a halt, joy and relief spiraling through him.

"I love you. I love you. I love you.'' Kate sang out, and was instantly rewarded with a kiss that stole her breath away.

"I think we should get married right away,'' Marsh said when he surfaced a few moments later.

Kate laughed softly. "I'd like that.''

"Ah…but I have to do this properly. First you'll need a ring.'' He brought her hand to his mouth, kissing her fingers one by one. "A diamond, I think. Yes, a diamond for Kate.''

"Oh, Marsh. You're the only Diamond I need,'' Kate said, her heart brimming over with love. Her dream of a family had come true at last and she was going to hold on to it with all her might.

* * * * *

Be sure to watch for Spencer's romance,
THE FAMILY DIAMOND, coming soon to
Silhouette Romance.

Coming from Silhouette Romance®:

Cinderella 👑 BRIDES

From rising star
ELIZABETH HARBISON

These women are about to live out their very own fairy tales...but will they live happily ever after?

On sale November 1999
EMMA AND THE EARL (SR #1410)

She thought she'd outgrown dreams of happily-ever-after, yet when American Emma Lawrence found herself a guest of Earl Brice Palliser's lavish estate, he seemed her very own Prince Charming.

On sale December 1999
PLAIN JANE MARRIES THE BOSS (SR #1416)

Sexy millionaire Trey Breckenridge III had finally asked Jane Miller to marry him. She knew he only needed a convenient wife to save his business, so Jane had just three months to show Trey the joys a forever wife could bring!

And look for the fairy tale to continue in January 2000 in **ANNIE AND THE PRINCE**.

Cinderella Brides, only from

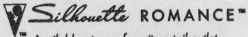

▼ *Silhouette* ROMANCE™

Available at your favorite retail outlet.

Visit us at www.romance.net

SRCBR

Don't miss Silhouette's newest cross-line promotion,

Four royal sisters find their own Prince Charmings as they embark on separate journeys to find their missing brother, the Crown Prince!

The search begins in October 1999 and continues through February 2000:

On sale October 1999: **A ROYAL BABY ON THE WAY** by award-winning author **Susan Mallery** (Special Edition)

On sale November 1999: **UNDERCOVER PRINCESS** by bestselling author **Suzanne Brockmann** (Intimate Moments)

On sale December 1999: **THE PRINCESS'S WHITE KNIGHT** by popular author **Carla Cassidy** (Romance)

On sale January 2000: **THE PREGNANT PRINCESS** by rising star **Anne Marie Winston** (Desire)

On sale February 2000: **MAN...MERCENARY...MONARCH** by top-notch talent **Joan Elliott Pickart** (Special Edition)

ROYALLY WED
Only in—
SILHOUETTE BOOKS

Available at your favorite retail outlet.

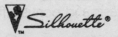

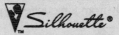

The clock is ticking for three brides-to-be in these three brand-new stories!

3, 2, 1... Married!

In this exciting collection of romantic tales, three marriage-minded women set their sights on becoming brides in time for the New Year.

How to hook a husband when time is of the essence?

Bestselling author **SHARON SALA** takes her heroine way out west, where the men are plentiful...and more than willing to make some lucky lady a "Miracle Bride."

Award-winning author **MARIE FERRARELLA** tells the story of a single woman searching for any excuse to visit the playground and catch sight of a member of "The Single Daddy Club."

Beloved author **BEVERLY BARTON** creates a heroine who discovers that personal ads are a bit like opening Door Number 3—the prize for "Getting Personal" may just be more than worth the risk!

On sale December 1999, at your favorite retail outlet.
Only from Silhouette Books!

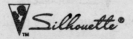

Silhouette®

Visit us at www.romance.net

PS321

**Start celebrating Silhouette's 20th anniversary
with these 4 special titles by
New York Times bestselling authors**

Fire and Rain
by Elizabeth Lowell

King of the Castle
by Heather Graham Pozzessere

State Secrets
by Linda Lael Miller

Paint Me Rainbows
by Fern Michaels

On sale in December 1999

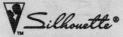

MONTANA MAVERICKS
Big Sky Brides

Legendary love comes to Whitehorn, Montana,
once more as beloved authors

Christine Rimmer, Jennifer Greene and Cheryl St.John

present three brand-new stories in this exciting anthology!

Meet the Brennan women:
SUZANNA, DIANA and ISABELLE

Strong-willed beauties who find unexpected
love in these irresistible marriage of
covnenience stories.

Don't miss
MONTANA MAVERICKS: BIG SKY BRIDES
On sale in February 2000,
only from Silhouette Books!

Available at your favorite retail outlet.

Silhouette®